THE CAMPFIRE GIRLS
SERIES

They had hearty appetites for the camp breakfast.

A Campfire Girl's Happiness

By
JANE L. STEWART

CAMPFIRE GIRLS SERIES
VOLUME VI

WILDSIDE PRESS

The Camp Fire Girls
At the Seashore

CHAPTER I

FROM THE ASHES

The sun rose over Plum Beach to shine down on a scene of confusion and wreckage that might have caused girls less determined and courageous than those who belonged to the Manasquan Camp Fire of the Camp Fire Girls of America to feel that there was only one thing to do—pack up and move away. But, though the camp itself was in ruins, there were no signs of discouragement among the girls themselves Merry laughter vied with the sound of the waves, and the confusion among the girls was more apparent than real.

"Have you got everything sorted, Margery—

the things that are completely ruined and those
that are worth saving?'' asked Eleanor Mercer,
the Guardian of the Camp Fire.

"Yes, and there's more here that we can save
and still use than anyone would have dreamed
just after we got the fire put out,'' replied Margery Burton, one of the older girls, who was a
Fire-Maker. In the Camp Fire there are three
ranks—the Wood-Gatherers, to which all girls
belong when they join; the Fire-Makers, next in
order, and, finally, the Torch-Bearers, of which
Manasquan Camp Fire had none These rank
next to the Guardian in a Camp Fire, and, as a
rule, there is only one in each Camp Fire She
is a sort of assistant to the Guardian, and, as the
name of the rank implies, she is supposed to hand
on the light of what the Camp Fire has given
her, by becoming a Guardian of a new Camp Fire
as soon as she is qualified

"What's next?'' cried Bessie King, who had
been working with some of the other girls in sort-
ing out the things which could be used, despite

the damage done by the fire that had almost wiped out the camp during the night.

"Why, we'll start a fire of our own!" said Eleanor. "There's no sort of use in keeping any of this rubbish, and the best way to get rid of it is just to burn it. All hands to work now, piling it up and seeing that there is a good draught underneath, so that it will burn up. We can get rid of ashes easily, but half-burned things are a nuisance."

"Where are we going to sleep to-night?" asked Dolly Ransom, ruefully surveying the places where the tents had stood. Only two remained, which were used for sleeping quarters by some of the girls.

"I'm more bothered about what we're going to eat," said Eleanor, with a laugh. "Do you realize that we've been so excited that we haven't had any breakfast? I should think you'd be starved, Dolly. You've had a busier morning than the rest of us, even."

"I *am* hungry, when I'm reminded of it," said

Dolly, with a comical gesture. "What ever are we going to do, Miss Eleanor?"

"I'm just teasing you, Dolly," said Eleanor. "Mr. Salters came over from Green Cove in his boat, when he saw the fire, to see if he couldn't help in some way, and he's gone in to Bay City. He'll be out pretty soon with a load of provisions, and as many other things as he can stuff into the *Sally S.*"

"Then we're really going to stay here?" said Bessie King

"We certainly are!" said Eleanor, her eyes flashing. "I don't see why we should let a little thing like this fire drive us away! We are going to stay here, and, what's more, we're going to have just as good a time as we planned to have when we came here—if not a better one!"

"Good!" cried half a dozen of the girls together.

Soon all the rubbish was collected, and a fire had been built. And, while Margery Burton applied a light to it, the girls formed a circle about it, and danced around, singing the while the most popular of Camp Fire songs, Wo-he-lo.

"That's like burning all the unpleasant things that have happened to us, isn't it?" said Eleanor. "We just toss them into the flames, and they're gone! What's left is clean and good and useful, and we will make all the better use of it for having lost what is burning now."

"Isn't it strange, Miss Eleanor," said Bessie King, "that this should have happened to us so soon after the fire that burned up the Pratt's farm?"

"Yes, it is," replied Eleanor. "And there's a lesson in it for us, just as there was for them in their fire. We didn't expect to find them in such trouble when we started to walk there, but we were able to help them, and to show them that there was a way of rising from the ruin of their home, and being happier and more prosperous than they had been before."

"We're going to do that, too," said Dolly, with spirit. "I felt terrible when I first saw the place in the light, after the fire was all out, but it looks different already.''

"Mr. Salters will be here soon," said Eleanor. "And now there's nothing more to do until he comes. We'll have a fine meal—and if you're half as hungry as I am you'll be glad of that—and we'll spend the afternoon in getting the place to rights. But just now the best thing for all of us to do is to rest."

"I'll be glad to do that," said Dolly Ransom, as she linked her arm with Bessie's and drew her away. "I am pretty tired."

"I should think you would be, Dolly. I haven't had a chance to thank you yet for what you did for me."

"Oh, nonsense, Bessie!" said Dolly, flushing. "You'd have done it for me, wouldn't you? I'm only just as glad as I can be that I was able to do anything to get you away from Mr. Holmes—you and Zara."

"Zara's gone to pieces completely, Dolly. She was terribly frightened—more than I was, I think, and yet I don't see how that can be, because I was as frightened as I think anyone could have been."

"I never saw them get hold of you at all, Bessie. How did it happen?"

"Well, that's pretty hard to say, Dolly. You know, after we found out that that yacht was here just to watch us, I was nervous, and so were you."

"I think we had reason to be nervous, don't you?"

"I should say so! Well, anyhow, as soon as I saw that the tents were on fire, I was sure that the men on the yacht had had something to do with it. But, of course, there wasn't anything to do but try as hard as I could to help put out the fire, and it was so exciting that I didn't think about any other danger until I saw a man from the boat that had come ashore pick Zara up and start to carry her out to it "

"They pretended to be helping us with the fire, and they really did help, Bessie I guess we wouldn't have saved any of the tents at all if it hadn't been for them."

6—C2

"Oh, I saw what they were doing! When I saw the man pick Zara up, though, I knew right away what their plan was. And I was just going to scream when another man got hold of me, and he kept me from shouting, and carried me off to the yacht in the boat. Zara had fainted, and they kept us down below in a cabin and said they were going to take us along the coast until we came to the coast of the state Zara and I were in when we met you girls first "

"We guessed that, Bessie. That was one of the things we were all worrying about when we came here—that they might try to carry you two off that way. I don't see how it can be that you're all right as long as you're in this state, and in danger as soon as you go back to the one you came from."

"Well, you see, Zara and I really did run away, I suppose. Zara's father is in prison, so they said she had to have a guardian, and I left the Hoovers. So that old Farmer Weeks—you know about him, don't you?—is our guardian in that

state, and he's got an order from the judge near
Hedgeville putting us in his care until we are
twenty-one.''

"But that order's no good in this state?''

"No, because here Miss Mercer is our guardian.
But if they can get us into that other state, no
matter how, they can hold us.''

"Oh, I see! And, of course, Miss Eleanor understood right away. When we told the men who
had helped us with the fire that you were missing,
they said they were afraid you must have been
caught in the fire, but Miss Eleanor said she was
sure you were on the yacht. And they just
laughed.''

"I heard that big man, Jeff, talking to her
when she went aboard the yacht.''

"Yes. They wouldn't let her look for you, and
he threatened to put her off if she didn't come
ashore. You heard that, didn't you?''

"Oh, yes! Zara and I could hear everything
she said when she was in the cabin on the yacht.
But we couldn't let her know where we were.''

"Well, just as soon as she could get to a telephone, Miss Eleanor called up Bay City, and asked them to send policemen or some sort of officers who could search the yacht. But we were terribly afraid that they would sail away before those men could get here, and then, you see, we couldn't have done a thing. There wouldn't have been any way of catching them."

"And they'd have done it, too, if it hadn't been for you, Dolly! I don't see how you ever thought of it, and how you were brave enough to do what you did when you did think of it."

"Oh, pshaw, Bessie—it was easy! I knew enough about yachts to understand that if their screw was twisted up with rope it wouldn't turn, and that would keep them there for a little while, anyhow. And they never seemed to think of that possibility at all. So I swam out there, and, of course, I could dive and stay down for a few seconds at a time. It was easier, because I had something to hold on to."

"It was mighty clever, and mighty plucky of you, too, Dolly."

"There was only one thing I regretted, Bessie. I wish I'd been able to hear what they said when they found out they couldn't get away!"

"I wish you'd been there, too, Dolly," said Bessie, laughing "They were perfectly furious, and everyone on board blamed everyone else. It took them quite a while to find out what was the matter, and then even after they found out, it meant a long delay before they could clear the screw and get moving"

"I never was so glad of anything in my life, Bessie, as when we saw the men from Bay City coming while that yacht was still here! We kept watching it all the time, of course, and we saw them send the sailor over to dive down and find out what was wrong. Then we could see him going down and coming up, time after time, and it seemed as if he would get it done in time."

"It must have been exciting, Dolly."

"I guess it was just as exciting for you, wasn't

it? But it would have been dreadful if, after
having held them so long, it hadn't been quite
long enough ''

"Well, it *was* long enough, Dolly, thanks to
you! I hate to think of where I would be now if
you hadn't managed it so cleverly."

"What will they do to those men on the yacht,
do you suppose?"

"I don't know. Miss Eleanor wants to
prove that it was Mr. Holmes who got them
to do it, I think. But that won't be decided
until her cousin, Mr. Jamieson, the lawyer,
comes. He'll know what we'd better do, and
I'm sure Miss Eleanor will leave it to him to
decide ''

"I tell you one thing, Bessie. This sort of per-
secution of you and Zara has got to be stopped.
I really do believe they've gone too far this time.
Of course, if they had got you away, they'd have
been all right, because in that other state where
you two came from what they did was all right.
But they got caught at it. I certainly do hope

that Mr. Jamieson will be able to find some way
to stop them ''

"I'm glad we're going to stay here, aren't you,
Dolly? Do you know, I really feel that we'll be
safer here now than if we went somewhere else?
They've tried their best to get at us here, and
they couldn't manage it. Perhaps now they'll
think that we'll be on our guard too much, and
leave us alone.''

"I hope so, Bessie. But look here, there were
two girls on guard last night, and what good did
it do us?''

"You don't think they were asleep, do you,
Dolly?''

"No, I'm sure they weren't But they just
didn't have a chance to do anything. What happened was this Margery and Mary were sitting
back to back, so that one could watch the yacht
and the other the path that leads up to the spring
on top of the bluff, where those two men we had
seen were sitting ''

"That was a good idea, Dolly.''

"First rate, but those people were too clever. They didn't row ashore in a boat—not here, at least And no one came down the path, until later, anyhow. The first thing that made Margery think there was anything wrong was when she smelt smoke and then, a second later, the big living tent was all ablaze."

"It might have been an accident, Dolly, I suppose—"

"Oh, yes, it might have been, but it wasn't! They were here too soon, and it fitted in too well with their plans Miss Eleanor thinks she knows how they started the fire "

"But how could they have done that, if there were none of them here on the beach, Dolly?"

"She says that if they were on the bluff, above the tents, they could very easily have thrown down bombs that would smoulder, and soon set the canvas on fire. And there was a high wind last night, and it wouldn't have taken long, once a spark had touched the canvas, for everything to blaze up. They couldn't have picked a much better night."

"I don't suppose that can be proved, though, Dolly."

"I'm afraid not. That's what Miss Eleanor says, too. She says you can often be so sure of a thing yourself that it seems that it must have happened, without being able to prove it to some-one else. That's where they are so clever, and that's what makes them so dangerous. They can hide their tracks splendidly."

"I don't see why men who can do such things couldn't keep straight, and really make more money honestly than they can by being crooked "

"It does seem strange, doesn't it, Bessie? Oh, look, there's the *Sally S.* with our breakfast— and there's another boat coming in I wonder if Mr. Jamieson can be here already ?"

In a moment his voice proved that it *was* possible, and a few minutes later, while the girls were helping Captain Salters to unload the stores he had brought with him, Eleanor was greeting her attorney from Bay City.

CHAPTER II

"I guess you haven't met Billy Trenwith properly yet, Eleanor," said Charlie Jamieson, smiling.

"Maybe not," said Eleanor, returning the smile, "but I regard him as a friend already, Charlie. He was splendid this morning. If he hadn't understood so quickly, and acted at once, the way he did, I don't know what would have happened."

"I'm afraid I didn't really understand at all, Miss Mercer," said Trenwith, a good looking young fellow, with light brown hair and grey blue eyes, that, although mild and pleasant enough now, had been as cold as steel when Bessie had seen him on the yacht. "But I could understand readily enough that you were in trouble, and I knew that Charlie's cousin wouldn't appeal to me

27

unless there was a good reason. So I didn't feel
that I was taking many chances in doing what
you wished.''

"I'm afraid you took more chances than you
know about, Billy," said Charlie, gravely.
"You're in politics, aren't you? And you have
ambitions for more of a job than you've got now?"

"Oh, yes, I'm in politics, after a fashion," admitted Trenwith. "But I guess I could manage
to keep alive if I never got another political office.
I had a bit of a practice before I became district
attorney, and I think I could build it up again."

"Well, I hope this isn't going to make any difference, Billy. But it's only fair for you to know
the sort of game you're running into. I don't
want to feel that you're going ahead to help us
without understanding the situation just as it is."

"You talk as if this might be a pretty compli-
cated bit of business, Charlie. Suppose you
loosen up and tell me about it. Then I may be
able to figure better on how I can help you "

"That's just what I'm going to do, old man.

I want you to meet two of cousin's protegees here —Bessie King and Zara, the mysterious. If we knew more about Zara and her affairs this wouldn't be such a Chinese puzzle. But here goes! Ask me all the questions you like. And you girls—if I go wrong, stop me.

"In the first place, Miss Mercer here took a party of her Camp Fire Girls, these same ones that you can see there so busy about getting breakfast, over the state line, and they went to a camp on a lake a little way from a village called Hedgeville."

"I know the place," nodded Trenwith. "Never been there, but I know where it is "

"Well, one morning they discovered these two —Bessie and Zara. And they'd had a strange experience. They were running away!"

"Bad business, as a rule," commented Trenwith. "But I suppose there was a good reason?"

"You bet there was, old chap! Bessie had lived for a good many years with an old farmer called Hoover and his wife. They had a son, too, a worthless young scamp named Jake, lazy and ready for any sort of mischief that turned up!''

"Is she related to them in any way, Charlie?"

"Not a bit of it! When she was a little bit of a kid her parents left her there as a boarder, and they were supposed to send money to pay for her keep until they came back to get her. For a while they did, but then the money stopped coming.''

"But they kept her on, just the same?"

"Yes, as a sort of unpaid servant. She did all the work she could manage, and she didn't have a very good time. Zara, here, has a father. How long ago did Zara and her father come to Hedgeville, Bessie?"

"They'd been there about two years when we—we had to run away, Mr. Jamieson. They came from some foreign country, you know."

"Yes. And the people around Hedgeville couldn't make much out about them, so they decided, of course, being unable to understand them, that there must be something wrong about Zara's dad. No real reason at all, except that he only spoke a little English, and liked to keep his business to himself.''

Trenwith laughed.

"I know," he said. "I see a lot of that sort of thing "

"Well, the day before the two of them ran away—or the day before they found the girls, rather—there'd been a fine shindy at the Hoovers. Zara went over to see Bessie, and Jake Hoover locked her in a tool shed. Then he managed, without meaning to do it, to set the tool shed afire, and said he was going to say that Bessie had done it."

"Fine young pup, he must be!"

"Yes—worth knowing! Anyhow, Bessie had only too good reason to know that his mother would believe him and take his word, no matter what she and Zara said. So, being scared, she just ran. I don't blame her! I'd have done the same thing myself. You and I both know that

knowing he's innocent doesn't keep a man who
is unjustly accused from being afraid.''

"No," said Trenwith, thoughtfully. "I've had
to learn that it doesn't pay to think a man's
guilty because he's scared and confused. It's
an old theory that innocence shows in a prisoner's eyes, and it's very pretty—only it isn't
true.''

"Well, even so, they might not have run away
if it hadn't happened that that was the day Zara's
father was arrested. Apparently with an old
miser and money lender called Weeks as the moving spirit, a charge of counterfeiting was cooked
up against him, and they took him off to my town
to jail.''

"But it's in another state!"

"United States case, you see. My town's the
centre of the Federal district. Zara and Bessie
happened to get on to this, and when they crept
up to Zara's house to find out if it was true, they
overheard enough to show them that it was—
and, what was more, that old Weeks meant to get

himself appointed Zara's guardian, and take her home with him."

"Oh, that was his game, eh?"

"Yes, and if you'd ever seen him, you wouldn't blame Zara for being ready to run away before she went with him. He's the meanest old codger you ever saw. But he had a big pull in that region, because he held mortgages on about all the farms, and he could do about as he liked."

"Well, I don't see why they didn't have a perfect right to run away," said Trenwith, "legally and morally. They didn't owe anything in the way of gratitude to any of these people."

"That's just what I said!" declared Eleanor, vehemently. "I looked into the story they told me, and I found out it was perfectly true. So we helped them, and took them into this state."

"Yes. And old Weeks chased them, and got Zara away from them once. Bessie tricked him and got her back," said Jamieson. "And then the old rip got a court order making him Zara's guardian, but he tried to serve it across the state

6—C3

line, and got dished for his trouble. So it looked as if they'd shaken him pretty well."

"I should say so! Do you mean that he kept it up after that?"

"He certainly did! And he got pretty powerful help too. Here's where the part of it that ought to interest you really begins. Miss Mercer took the two girls home with her, and almost at once, in the middle of the night, Zara was spirited away. At first we thought she'd been kidnapped but later it turned out that she'd been deceived, and gone with them willingly."

"This is beginning to sound pretty exciting, Charlie."

"I got interested in the case, Billy, and I tried to do what I could for Zara's father. He didn't trust me much, and I had a dickens of a time persuading him to talk. And then, just as I was about on the point of succeeding, he shut up like a clam, fired me as his lawyer, and hired Isaac Brack!"

"That little shyster? Good Heavens!"

"Right! Well, she—Zara, I mean—seemed to
have vanished into thin air. We couldn't get any
trace of her at all, until Bessie here dug up a
wild idea that it was in Morton Holmes's car she'd
been taken off."

"Holmes, the big dry goods merchant?" said
Trenwith, with a laugh. "How in the world did
she ever get such a wild idea as that? He wouldn't
be mixed up in anything shady!"

"Just what we told her," said Charlie, un-
smilingly, "but she insisted she was right. And,
a little while later, after Miss Mercer had taken
the girls to her father's farm, Holmes came along,
tricked her into getting in his car with another
girl, and ran them over the state line. He met
Weeks and this Jake Hoover—but Bessie was too
smart for them, and got back over the state line
safely. And the same day, putting two and two
together, I found Zara, held a prisoner in an old
house that Holmes had bought!"

"Good Lord!" said Trenwith, blankly. "So
Holmes had been in it from the start?"

"I don't know how long he's been mixed up in it, but he was in it then, with both feet. He was hand in glove with old Weeks, and for some reason he was mighty anxious to get both the girls across the state line and into old Weeks's care as guardian appointed by one of their courts over there."

"But why, Charlie—why?"

"I wish I knew. I've been cudgelling my brains for weeks to get the answer to that question, Billy. It's kept me awake nights, and I'm no nearer to it now than I was at the beginning. But hold on, you haven't heard it all yet, by a good deal!"

"What? Do you mean they weren't content with that?"

"Not so that you could notice it, they weren't! The girls went to Long Lake, up in the woods, and while they were there, a gypsy tried to carry them off. He mixed them up a bit, and, partly by good luck, and partly by Bessie's good nerve and pluck, he was caught and landed in jail at Hamilton, the county seat up there."

"Was Holmes mixed up in that?"

"Yes. He'd been fool enough to write a letter to the gypsy, and sign his own name to it. He hired lawyers to defend the gypsy, too, but that letter smashed his case, and the gypsy went to jail. They were afraid of Holmes, though, at Hamilton and we couldn't touch him. He's got a whole lot of money and power, too, especially in politics. So he can get away with things that would land a smaller man in jail in a jiffy."

"His money and pull won't do him any good down here," said Trenwith, his eyes snapping. "Have you any reason to think he was mixed up in this outrage here this morning and last night, Charlie?"

"Every reason to think so, Billy, but mighty little proof to back up what I think. There's the rub. Still—well, we'll see what we see later. I'll give you some of the reasons."

"You'd better," said Trenwith, grimly. "I think it's pretty nearly time for me to take a hand in this." He shot a look at Eleanor that

Bessie did not fail to notice. Evidently her charms had already made an impression on him.

"Yesterday, when Miss Mercer brought the girls down to Bay City from Windsor," Jamieson went on, "the train was to stop for a minute at Canton, which, though they had none of them thought of it, is in Weeks's state. And Bessie happened to discover that Jake Hoover was spying on them. She stayed behind the others at Windsor, discovered that he was telegraphing the news to Holmes, and guessed the plot."

"Good for her!" exclaimed Trenwith.

"So she got a message through to Miss Mercer on the train, and, being warned, Zara was able to elude the people who searched the train for her at Canton. Bessie went on a later train that didn't stop at Canton at all, so they were all right."

"That looks like pretty good evidence," said Trenwith, frowning. "He knew they were coming here and he'd made one attempt to get hold of them on the way."

"Yes, and there's more. When this yacht turned up here last night, Miss Mercer and the girls were nervous. And Bessie and her chum Dolly Ransom happened to overhear two men who were put at the top of that bluff to watch the camp. They talked about the 'boss' and how he meant to get those girls and had been 'stung once too often.' But they didn't mention Holmes by name "

"Too bad. Still, that fire was too timely to have been accidental. I think maybe we can convict them of starting it Then if these fellows think they're in danger of going to prison, we might offer them a chance of liberty if they confess and implicate Holmes, de you see?"

"It would be a good bargain, Billy."

"That's what I think. I'd let the tool escape any time to get hold of the man who was using him. They and the yacht are held safely at Bay City, in any case, and we have plenty of time to decide what's best to be done there."

"If I know Holmes, he'll show you his hand pretty soon, Bill I believe he thinks that every man has his price, and he probably has an idea that he can get you on his side if he works it right and offers you enough "

"He's got several more thinks coming on that," said Trenwith, angrily. "What a hound he must be! We've got to get to the bottom of this business, Charlie. That's all there is to it!"

"Won't Jake Hoover help, Charlie? ' suggested Eleanor. "He told Bessie he would go in to see you "

"He did come, but I was called away, and meant to talk to him again this morning, Nell. Then of course I had to come down here when I got this news from you and so I didn't have a chance. But I may get something out of him yet."

"We've decided, Mr. Trenwith," Eleanor explained, "that the reason Jake is doing just what they want is that he's afraid of them—that they know of some wrong thing he has done, and have been threatening to expose him if he doesn't obey them.''

"Well, if they're scaring him," said Charlie, "the thing for us to do is to scare him worse than they can. He'll stick to the side he's most afraid of.''

"Let's get him down here," said Trenwith. "Then we can not only handle him better, but we can keep an eye on him. I'm with you in this, Charlie, for anything I can do.''

"Good man!" said Charlie "Then you're not afraid of Holmes? He's pretty powerful, you know."

Trenwith looked at Eleanor. And when he saw the smile she gave him, and her look of liking and of confidence, he laughed.

"I guess I can look after myself," he said. "No, I'm not afraid of him, old man! We'll fight this out together.''

CHAPTER III

"I like that Mr. Trenwith, Bessie," said Dolly, when the meal was over and she and Bessie were working together. They usually managed to arrange their work so that they could be together at it.

"So do I, Dolly. He doesn't seem to be a bit afraid of Mr. Holmes, and I do believe he will help Mr. Jamieson an awful lot."

"I guess he'll need help, all right," said Dolly, gravely. "The more I think about that fire, the more scared I get. Why, how did those wretches know that some of us wouldn't be hurt?"

"I guess they didn't, Dolly."

"Then they simply didn't care, that's all. And isn't that dreadful, Bessie? The idea of doing such a thing!"

"I wish we knew why they did it, or why Mr.

43

Holmes wants them to do such things. It's easy enough to see why *they* did it—they wanted the money he had promised to pay if they got Zara and me away from here.''

"You remember what I told you. Mr. Holmes expects to make a lot of money out of you two, in some fashion. I know you laughed at me when I said that before, and said he had so much money already that that couldn't be the reason. But there simply can't be any other, Bessie; that's all there is to it.''

Bessie sighed wearily.

"I wish it was all over," she said. "Sometimes I'm sorry they haven't caught me and taken me back ''

"Why, Bessie, that's an awful thing for you to say! Don't you want to be with us?''

"Of course I do, Dolly! I've never been so happy in my whole life as I have been since that morning when I saw you girls for the first time. But I hate to think of the trouble my staying makes, and when I think that maybe there's danger for the rest of you, as there was last night—"

"Don't you worry about that, Bessie! I guess we can stand it if you can. That's what friends are for—to share your troubles. You mustn't get to feeling that way—it's silly"

"Well, it doesn't make much difference, Dolly. I don't seem to be able to help it. But I wish it was all over   And do you know what worries me most of all?"

"No.   What?"

"Why, what that nasty lawyer, Isaac Brack, said to me one time. Do you remember my telling you? That unless I went with him, and did what he and his friends wanted, I'd never find out about my father and my mother."

"I don't believe it, Bessie! I don't believe he knows anything at all about them, and I don't believe, either, that that's the only way you'll ever hear anything about them."

"But it might be true!"

"Oh, come on, Bessie, cheer up! You're going

to be all right. And I'll bet that when you do find
out about your parents, and why they left you
with Maw Hoover so long, you'll be glad you had
to wait so long, because it will make you so happy
when you do know.''

Just then Eleanor's voice called the girls together.

"All hands to work rebuilding the camp," she
said. "We want to have the new tents set up,
and everything ready for the night. I'd like
those people to know, if they come snooping
around here again, that it takes more than a fire
to put the Camp Fire Girls out of business!"

"My, but you're a slave driver, Nell," said
Charlie Jamieson, jovially. He winked in the
direction of Trenwith. "I'm sorry for your husband when you get married. You'll keep him
busy, all right!"

Hearing the remark, Trenwith grinned, while
Eleanor flushed. His look said pretty plainly
that he wouldn't waste any sympathy on the man
lucky enough to marry Eleanor Mercer, and

Dolly, catching the look, drew Bessie aside. Her observation in such matters was amazingly keen.

"Did you see that?" she whispered, excitedly. "Why, Bessie, I do believe he's fallen in love with her already!"

"Well, I should think he would!" said Bessie, surprisingly. "I wouldn't think much of any man who didn't! She's the nicest girl I ever saw or dreamed of seeing."

"Oh, she's all of that," agreed Dolly, loyally. "You can't tell me anything nice about Miss Eleanor that I haven't found out for myself long ago. But Mr. Jamieson isn't in love with her— and he's known her much longer than Mr. Trenwith has."

"That hasn't got anything at all to do with it," declared Bessie. "People don't have to know one another a long time to fall in love—though sometimes they don't always know about it themselves right away. And, besides, I think she and Mr. Jamieson are just like brother and sister. They're only cousins, of course, but they've sort of grown up together, and they know one another awfully well."

"You may know more about things like that than I do," agreed Dolly, dubiously. "But I know this much, anyhow. If I were a man, I'd certainly be in love with Miss Eleanor, if I knew her at all."

She stopped for a moment to look at Eleanor.

"Better not let her catch us whispering about her," she went on "She wouldn't like it a little bit."

"It isn't a nice thing to do anyhow, Dolly. You're perfectly right. I do think Mr. Trenwith's a nice man. Maybe he's good enough for her. But I think I'll always like Mr. Jamieson better, because he's been so nice to us from the very start, when he knew that we couldn't pay him, the way people usually do lawyers who work so hard for them "

"He certainly is a nice man, Bessie. But then so is Mr. Trenwith."

"Look out, Dolly!" cautioned Bessie, with a

low laugh. "You'll be getting jealous and losing your temper first thing you know"

"Oh, I guess not. Talking about losing one's temper, I wonder if Gladys Cooper is still mad at us?"

"Oh, I hope not! That was sort of funny, wasn't it, as well as unpleasant? Why do you suppose she was so angry, and got the other girls in their camp at Lake Dean to hating us so much when we first went there?"

"Oh, she couldn't help it, Bessie, I guess. It's the way she's been brought up. Her people have lots of money, and they've let her think that just because of that she is better than girls whose parents are poor."

"Well, the rest of them certainly changed their minds about us, didn't they?"

"Yes, and it was a fine thing! I guess they realized that we were better than they thought, when Gladys and Marcia Bates got lost in the woods that time, and you and I happened to find them, and get them home safely"

"I think they were mighty nice girls, Dolly— much nicer than you would ever have thought they could be from the way they acted when we first met them, and they ordered us off their ground, just as if we were going to hurt it. When they found out that they'd been in the wrong, and hadn't behaved nicely, they said they were sorry, and admitted that they hadn't been nice. And I think that's a pretty hard thing for anyone to do."

"Oh, it is, Bessie. I know, because I've found out so often that I'd been mean to people who were ever so much nicer than I. But there's one thing about it—it makes you feel sort of good all over when you have owned up that way. I wish Gladys Cooper had acted like the rest of them. But she was still mad "

"Oh, I think you'll find she's all right when you see her again, Dolly. I guess she's just as nice as the rest of them, really."

"That's one reason I'm sorry she acted that way. Because she's as nice as any girl you ever

saw when she wants to be. I was awfully mad at
her when it happened, but now, somehow, I've
got over feeling that way about her, altogether,
and I just want to be good friends with her again.''

"You lose your temper pretty quickly, Dolly,
but you get over being angry just as quickly as
you get mad, don't you?''

"I seem to, Bessie And I guess that's helping
me not to get angry at people so much, anyhow.
I'm always sorry when I do get into one of my
rages, and if I'm going to be sorry, it's easier
not to get mad in the first place.''

While they talked, Bessie and Dolly were not
idle, by any means. There was plenty of work
for everyone to do, for the fire had made a pretty
clean sweep, after all, and to put the whole camp
in good shape, so that they could sleep there that
night, was something of a task.

Trenwith and Jamieson, laughing a good deal,
and enjoying themselves immensely, insisted on
doing the heavy work of setting up the ridge
poles, and laying down the floors of the new tents,

but when it came to stretching the canvas over the framework, they were not in it with the girls.

"You men mean well, but I never saw anything so clumsy in my life!" declared Eleanor, laughingly. "It's a wonder to me how you ever come home alive when you go out camping by yourselves."

"Oh, we manage somehow," boasted Charlie Jamieson.

"That's just about what you do do! You manage—somehow! And, yet, when this Camp Fire movement started, all the men I knew sat around and jeered, and said that girls were just jealous of the good times the Boy Scouts had, and predicted that unless we took men along to look after us, we'd be in all sorts of trouble the first time we ever undertook to spend a night in camp!"

Charlie shook his head at Trenwith in mock alarm.

"Getting pretty independent, aren't they?" he said to his friend. "You mark my words,

Billy, the old-fashioned women don't exist any more!"

"And it's a good thing if they don't!" Eleanor flashed back at him. "They do, though, only you men don't know the real thing when you see it. You have an idea that a woman ought to be helpless and clinging Maybe that was all right in the old days, when there were always plenty of men to look after a woman. But how about the way things are now? Women have to go into shops and offices and factories to earn a living, don't they, just the way men do?"

"They do—more's the pity!" said Trenwith.

Eleanor looked at him as if she understood just what he meant

"Maybe it isn't so much of a pity, though," she said "I tell you one thing—a girl isn't going to make any the worse wife for being self-reliant, and knowing how to take care of herself a little bit. And that's what we want to make of our Camp Fire Girls—girls who can help themselves if there's need for it, and who don't need to have

a man wasting a lot of time doing things for them
that he ought to be spending in serious work—
things that she can do just as well for herself.''

She stood before them as she spoke, a splendid
figure of youth, and health and strength. And, as
she spoke, she plunged her hand into a capacious
pocket in her skirt.

"There!" she said, "that's one of the things
that has kept women helpless. It wasn't fashionable to have pockets, so men got one great advantage just in their clothes. Camp Fire Girls
have pockets!"

"You say that as if it was some sort of a motto,"
said Charlie, laughing, but impressed.

"It is!" she replied. "Camp Fire Girls have
pockets! That's one of the things you'll see in
any Camp Fire book you read—any of the books
that the National Council issues, I mean."

"I surrender! I'm converted—absolutely!"
said Jamieson, with a laugh. "I'll admit right
now that no lot of men or boys I know could have
put this camp up in this shape in such a time.

Why, hullo—what's that? Looks as if you were going to have neighbors, Nell "

His exclamation drew all eyes to the other end of the cove, and the surprise was general when a string of wagons was seen coming down a road that led to the beach from the bluff at that point.

"Looks like a camping party, all right," said Trenwith "Wonder who they can be?"

Eleanor looked annoyed. She remembered only too well and too vividly the disturbance that had followed the coming of the yacht, and she wondered if this new invasion of the peace of Plum Beach might not likewise be the forerunner of something unpleasant.

"They've got tents," she said, peering curiously at the wagons. "See—they're stopping there, and beginning to unload."

"They're doing themselves very well, whoever they are," said Trenwith "That's a pretty luxurious looking camp outfit. And they're having their work done for them by men who know the business, too."

"Yes, and they're not making a much better job of it than these girls did," said Charlie. "Great Scott! Look at those cases of canned goods! They've got enough stuff there to feed a regiment."

"Oh, I'm sorry they're coming!" said Eleanor, "whoever they are! I don't want to seem nasty, but we were ever so happy last summer when we were here quite alone."

"These people won't bother you, Nell," said Jamieson.

"You don't suppose this could be another trick of Mr. Holmes's, do you, Charlie?"

"Hardly—so soon," he said, frowning.

"He didn't leave us in peace very long after we got here, you know. We only arrived yesterday—and see what happened to us last night!"

"Well, we might stroll over and have a look," suggested Trenwith. "I guess there aren't any private property rights on this beach. We'll just look them over."

"All right," said Eleanor. "Want to come,

Dolly and Bessie? I see you've finished your share of the work before the others."

So the five of them walked over

"Who's going to camp here?" Trenwith asked one of the workmen

"I don't know, sir. We just got orders to set up the tents That's all we know about it."

The three girls exchanged glances. That sounded as if it might indeed be Mr. Holmes who was coming But before any more questions could be asked, there was a sudden peal of girlish laughter from above and a wild rush down from the bluff.

"Dolly Ransom! Isn't this a surprise? And didn't we tell you we had a surprise for you?"

"Why, Marcia Bates!" cried Dolly and Bessie, in one breath, as the newcomer reached them. "I didn't know you were going to leave Lake Dean so soon "

"Well, we did! And we're all here—Gladys Cooper, and all the Halsted Camp Girls!"

CHAPTER IV

In a moment the rest of the Halsted girls had reached the beach and were gathered about Bessie and Dolly. There was a lot of laughter and excitement, but it was plain that the girls who had once so utterly despised the members of the Camp Fire were now heartily and enthusiastically glad to see them. And suddenly Eleanor gave a glad cry.

"Why, Mary Turner!" she said. "Whatever are you doing here? I thought you were going to Europe!"

"I was, until this cousin of mine"—she playfully tapped Marcia on the shoulder—"made me change my plans. I'll have you to understand that you're not the only girl who can be a Camp Fire Guardian, Eleanor Mercer!"

"Well," gasped Eleanor, "of all things! Do

59

you mean that you've organized a new **Camp Fire?**"

"We certainly have—the Halsted Camp Fire, if you please! We're not really all in yet, but we've got permission now from the National Council, and the girls are to get their rings to-night at our first ceremonial camp fire. Won't you girls come over and help us?"

"I should say we would!" said Eleanor. "Why, this is fine, Mary! Tell me how it happened, won't you?"

"It's all your fault—you must know that. The girls have told me all about the horrid way they acted at Lake Dean, but really, you can't blame them so much, can you, Nell? It's the way they're brought up—and, well, you went to the school, too, just as I did!"

"I know what you mean," said Eleanor. "It's a fine school, but—"

"That's it exactly—that *but*. The school has got into bad ways, and these girls were in a fair way to be snobs. Well, Marcia and some of the others got to thinking things over, and they decided that if the Camp Fire had done so much for Dolly Ransom and a lot of your girls, it would be a good thing for them, too."

"They're perfectly right, Mary. Oh, I'm ever so glad!"

"So they came to me, and asked me if I wouldn't be their Guardian I didn't want to at first—and then I was afraid I wouldn't be any good. But I promised to talk to Mrs Chester, and get her to suggest someone who would do, and—"

"You needn't tell me the rest," laughed Eleanor "I know just what happened Mrs. Chester just talked to you in that sweet, gentle way of hers, and the first thing you knew you felt about as small as a pint of peanuts, and as if refusing to do the work would be about as mean as stealing sheep Now, didn't you?"

Mary laughed a little ruefully.

"You're just right! That's exactly how it happened," she said. "She told me that no one would be able to do as much with these girls as I could, and then, when she had me feeling properly ashamed of myself, she turned right around and began to make me see how much fun I would have out of it myself. So I talked to Miss Halsted, and made her go to see Mrs. Chester—and here we are!''

Suddenly Eleanor collapsed weakly against one of the empty packing boxes that littered the place, and began to laugh.

"Oh, my dear," she exclaimed, "if you only knew the awful things we were thinking about you before we knew who you were!"

"Why? Do you mean to say that you're snobbish, too, and didn't want neighbors you didn't know? Like my girls at Lake Dean?"

"No, but we thought you might be kidnappers, or murderers, or fire-bugs, like our last neighbors!"

"Eleanor! Are you crazy—and if you're not, what on earth are you talking about?"

"I'm not as crazy as I seem to be, Mary. It's only fair to tell you now that this beach may be a

pretty troubled spot while we're here. We seem
to attract trouble just as a magnet attracts iron.''

"I think you *are* crazy, Nell. If you're not,
won't you explain what you mean?''

"Look at our camp over there, Mary. It's
pretty solid and complete, isn't it?''

"I only hope ours looks half as well."

"Well, this morning at sunrise there were just
two tents standing. Everything else had been
burnt. And I was doing my best to get the police
or someone from Bay City to rescue two of my
girls who were prisoners on a yacht out there in
the cove!''

Mary Turner appealed whimsically to Charlie
Jamieson.

"Does she mean it, Charlie?'' she begged. "Or
is she just trying to string me?''

"I'm afraid she means it, and I happen to know
it's all true, Mary,'' said Charlie, enjoying her
bewilderment "But it's a long story. Perhaps
you'd better let it keep until you have put things
to rights.''

"We'll help in doing that," said Eleanor. "Dolly, run over and get the other girls, won't you? Then we'll all turn in and lend a hand, and it will all be done in no time at all."

"Indeed you won't!" said Marcia. "We're going to do everything ourselves, just to show that we can."

"There isn't much to do," said Mary Turner, with a laugh "So you needn't act as if that were something to be proud of, Marcia. You see, I thought it was better to take things easily at the start, Eleanor. They wanted to come here with all the tents and things and set up the camp by themselves, but I decided it was better to have the harder work done by men who knew their business "

"You were quite right, too," agreed Eleanor. "That's the way I arranged things for our own camp the day we came. To-day we did do the work ourselves, but there was a reason for the girls were so excited and nervous about the fire

that I thought it was better to give them a chance
to work off their excitement that way."

"I'm dying to hear all about the fire and what
has happened here," said Mary. "But I suppose
we'd better get everything put to rights first."

And, though the girls of the new Camp Fire
insisted on doing all the actual work themselves,
they were glad enough to take the advice of the
Manasquan girls in innumerable small matters.
Comfort, and even safety from illness, in camp
life, depends upon the observance of many seem-
ingly trifling rules

Gladys Cooper, who, more than any of her
companions at Camp Halsted, had tried to make
things unpleasant for the Manasquan girls at Lake
Dean, had not been with the first section of the
new Camp Fire to reach the beach. Dolly had
inquired about her rather anxiously, for Gladys
had not taken part in the general reconciliation
between the two parties of girls

"Gladys?" Marcia said. "Oh, yes, she's coming She's back in the wagon that's bringing our

suit cases We appointed her a sort of rear guard. It wouldn't do to lose those things, you know.''

"I was afraid—I sort of thought she might not want to come here if she knew we were here, Marcia. You know—''

"Yes, I *do* know, Dolly. She behaved worse than any of us, and she wasn't ready to admit it when you girls left Lake Dean. But she's come to her senses since then, I'm sure. The rest of us made her do that.''

Bessie King looked a little dubious.

"I hope you didn't bother her about it, Marcia,'' she said. "You know we haven't anything against her. We were sorry she didn't like us, and understand that we only wanted to be friends, but we certainly didn't feel angry.''

"If she was bothered, as you call it, Bessie, it served her good and right,'' said Marcia, crisply. "We've had about enough of Gladys and her superior ways. She isn't any better or cleverer or prettier than anyone else, and it's time she stopped giving herself airs.''

"You don't understand," said Bessie, with a smile. "She's one of you, and if you don't like the way she acts, you've got a perfect right to let her know it, and make her just as uncomfortable as you like."

"We did," said Marcia. "I guess she's had a lesson that will teach her it doesn't pay to be a snob."

"Yes, but don't you think that's something a person has to learn for herself, without anyone to teach her, Marcia? I mean, there's only one reason why she could be nice to us, and that's because she likes us. And you can't make her like us by punishing her for not liking us. You'll only make her hate us more than ever"

"She'll behave herself, anyhow, Bessie. And that's more than she did before."

"That's true enough But really, it would be better, if she didn't like us, for her to show it frankly than to go around with a grudge against us she's afraid to show. Don't you see that she'll blame us for making trouble between you girls

and her? She'll think that we've set her own
friends against her. Really, Marcia, I think all
the trouble would be ended sooner, in the long run,
if you just let her alone until she changed her
mind   She'll do it, sooner or later "

"I guess Bessie's right, Marcia," said Dolly,
thoughtfully. "I don't see why Gladys acts this
way, but I do think that the only thing that will
make her act differently will be for her to feel
differently, and nothing you can do will do that "

"Well, it's too late now, anyhow," said Marcia   "I see what you mean, and I suppose you
really are right. But it's done. You'll be nice to
her, won't you? She's promised to be pleasant
when she sees you—to talk to you, and all that. I
don't know how well she'll manage, but I guess
she'll do her best."

"There's no reason why we shouldn't be nice
to her   said Bessie. "She isn't hurting us. I
only hope that something will happen so that we
can be good friends."

"She really is a nice girl," said Marcia, "and

I'm awfully fond of her when she isn't in one of her tantrums But she is certainly hard to get along with when everything isn't going just to suit her little whims.''

"Here she comes now," said Dolly "I'm going to meet her."

"Well, you certainly did give us a surprise, Gladys," cried Dolly. "You sinner, why didn't you tell us what you were going to do?"

"Oh, hello, Dolly!" said Gladys, coolly. "I didn't see much of you at Lake Dean, you know. You were too busy with your—new friends "

"Oh, come off, Gladys!" said Dolly, irritated despite her determination to go more than half way in re-establishing friendly relations with Gladys "Why can't you be sensible? We've got more to forgive than you have, and we're willing to be friends. Aren't you going to behave decently?"

"I don't think I know just what you mean, Dolly," said Gladys, stiffly. "As long as the other girls have decided to be friendly with your—

friends, I am not going to make myself unpleasant. But you can hardly expect me to like people just because you do. I must say that 1 get along better with girls of my own class.''

"I ought to be mad at you, Gladys,'' said Dolly, with a peal of laughter ''But you're too funny! What do you mean by girls of your own class? Girls whose parents have as much money as yours? Mine haven't So I suppose I'm not in your class ''

"Nonsense, Dolly!'' said Gladys, angrily. "You know perfectly well I don't mean anything of the sort. I—I can't explain just what I mean by my own class—but you know it just as well as I do ''

"I think I know it better, Gladys,'' said Dolly, gravely "Now don't get angry, because I'm not saying this to be mean. If you had to go about with girls of your own class you couldn't stand them for a week! Because they'd be snobbish and mean. They'd be thinking all the time about how much nicer their clothes were than yours, or the other way around. They wouldn't have a good

word for anyone—they'd just be trying to think
about the mean things they could say!"

"Why, Dolly! What do you mean?"

"I mean that that's your class—the sort you
are. Our girls, in the Manasquan Camp Fire,
and most of the Halsted girls, are in a class a
whole lot better than yours, Gladys. They spend
their time trying to be nice, and to make other
people happy There isn't any reason why you
shouldn't improve, and get into their class, but
you're not in it now."

"I never heard of such a thing, Dolly! Do you
mean to tell me that you and I aren't in a better
class socially than these girls you're camping
with?"

"I'm not talking about society—and you
haven't any business to be. You don't know anything about it. But if people are divided into real
classes, the two big classes are nice people and
people who aren't nice. And each of those classes
is divided up again into a lot of other classes.
I hope I'm in as good a class as Bessie King and

Margery Burton, but I'm pretty sure I'm not.
And I know you're not "

"There's no use talking to you, Dolly," said
Gladys, furiously. "I thought you'd had time
to get over all that nonsense, but I see you're
worse than ever. I'm perfectly willing to be
friends with you, and I've forgiven you for throwing those mice at us at Lake Dean, but I certainly
don't see why I should be friendly with all those
common girls in your camp "

"They're not common—and don't you dare to
say they are! And you certainly can't be my
friend if you're going to talk about them that
way."

"All right!" snapped Gladys. "I guess I can
get along without your friendship if you can get
along without mine!"

"I didn't mean to," she said, disgustedly, to
Bessie and Marcia, "but I'm afraid I've simply
made her madder than ever. And there's no
telling what she'll do now!"

"Oh, I guess there's nothing to worry about,"

said Marcia, cheerfully enough. "We can keep
her in order all right, and if she doesn't behave
herself decently I guess you'll find that Miss
Turner will send her home in a hurry."

"Oh, I hope not," said Bessie. "That wouldn't
really do any good, would it? We want to be
friends with her—not to have any more trouble."

"I wish I'd kept out of it," said Dolly, dole-
fully. "I think I can keep my temper, and then I
go off and make things worse than ever! I ought
to know enough not to interfere. I'm like the
elephant that killed a little mother bird by accident, and he was so sorry that he sat on its nest to
hatch the eggs!"

"Maybe it's a good thing," said Marcia, laughing at the picture of the elephant. "After all,
isn't it a good deal as Bessie said? If there's bad
feeling, it's better to have it open and above-
board. We all know where we are now, anyhow.
And I certainly hope that something will turn up
to change her mind."

CHAPTER V

THE COUNCIL FIRE

"I hope it will, Bessie," said Dolly "But you know what a nasty temper I've got If she keeps on talking the way she has, I don't know what I'll say."

"Well, you might as well say what you like, Dolly. I believe she wants a good quarrel with someone—and it might as well be you."

"You mean you think she likes me to get angry?"

"Of course she does! There wouldn't be any fun in it for her if you didn't Can't you see that?"

Dolly looked very thoughtful.

"Then I won't give her the satisfaction of getting angry!" she declared, finally. "Of course you're right, Bessie. If we didn't pay any attention at all to her it wouldn't do her a bit of good to get angry, would it?"

"I wondered how long it would take you to see that, Dolly "

They were walking back to their own tents as they spoke. Once arrived there, neither said anything about the spirit Gladys had shown They both felt that it would be as well to let the other girls think that Gladys shared the friendly feelings of the other Halsted girls. And since Bessie and Dolly happened to be the only ones who knew that Gladys had been the prime mover in the trouble that had been made at Lake Dean, it was easy enough to conceal the true facts.

"She can't do anything by herself," said Dolly. "Up at Lake Dean nothing would have happened unless the rest of those girls had taken her part against us "

"I'm going to try to forget about her altogether, Dolly," said Bessie. "I'm not a bit angry at her, but if she won't be friends, she won't and that's all there is to it. And I don't see why I should worry about her when there are so many nice girls who *do* want to be friendly. Why, what are you laughing at?"

"I'm just thinking of how mad Gladys would be if she really understood! She's made herself think that she is doing a great favor to people when she makes friends of them—and, if she only knew it, she would have a hard time having us for friends now."

* * * * * * *

Charlie Jamieson and Billy Trenwith accepted Eleanor's pressing invitation to stay for the evening meal, but Trenwith seemed to feel that they were wasting time that might be better spent.

"Not wasting it exactly," he said, however, when Eleanor laughingly accused him of feeling so. "But I do sort of think that Charlie and I ought to keep after this man Holmes He seems to be a tough customer, and I'll bet he's busy, all right "

"The only point, Billy," said Charlie, "is that, no matter how busy we were, there's mighty little we could do We don't know enough, you see.

But maybe when I get up to the city, I'll find out more. I'll go over the facts with you in Bay City to-night, and then I'll go up to town and see what I can do with Jake Hoover and Zara's father.''

"Well, let's do something, for Heaven's sake!" said Trenwith. "I hate to think that all you girls out here are in danger as a result of this man's villainy. If he does anything rotten, I can see that he's punished but that might not do you much good."

"I tell you what would do some good, and that's to let Holmes know that you will punish him, if he exposes himself to punishment," said Charlie Jamieson. "That's the chief reason he's so bold. He thinks he's above the law—that he can do anything, and escape the consequences."

"Well, of course," said Trenwith, "it may enlighten him a bit when he finds that those rascals we caught to-day will have to stand trial, just as if they were friendless criminals. If what you say about him is so, he'll be after me to-morrow, trying to call me off. And I guess he'll find that he's up against the law for once."

"Did you get that telephone fixed up, Nell?" asked Charlie. "You're a whole lot safer with a telephone right here on the beach. Being half a mile from the nearest place where you can ever call for help is bad business."

Eleanor pointed to a row of poles, on which a wire was strung, leading into the main living tent.

"There it is," she said, gaily. "I don't see how you got them to do it so fast, though."

"Billy's a sort of political boss round here, as well as district attorney," laughed Jamieson. "When he says a thing's to be done, and done in a hurry, he usually has his way."

Eleanor looked curiously at Trenwith, and Charlie, catching the glance, winked broadly at Dolly Ransom. It was perfectly plain that the young District Attorney interested Eleanor a good deal. His quiet efficiency appealed to her. She liked men who did things, and Trenwith was es-

sentially of that type He didn't talk much about
his plans; he let results speak for him. And. at
the same time, when there was a question of something to be done, what he did say showed a quiet
confidence, which, while not a bit boastful, proved
that he was as sure of himself as are most competent men.

Also, his admiration for Eleanor was plain and
undisguised Charlie Jamieson, who was almost
like a brother in his relations with Eleanor, was
hugely amused by this. Somehow cousins who are
so intimate with a girl that they take a brother's
place, never do seem able to understand that she
may have the same attraction for other men that
the sisters and the cousins of the other men have
for them. The idea that their friends may fall
in love with the girls they regard in such a perfectly matter-of-fact way strikes them, when it
reaches them at all, as a huge joke.

All the girls were sorry to see the two men who
had helped them so much go away after dinner,
but of course their departure was necessary. Just

now, after the exciting events of the previous
night, there seemed a reasonable chance of a little
peace, but the price of freedom from the annoy-
ance caused by Holmes was constant vigilance, and
there was work for both the men to do. Moreover, the sight of the cheerful fire from the other
camp, and the thought of the great camp fire they
were presently to enjoy in common consoled them.

"The Halsted girls are going to build the fire,"
said Eleanor. "It's their first ceremonial camp
fire, so I told Miss Turner they were welcome to
do it. They're all Wood-Gatherers, you see. So
we'll have to light the fire for them, anyhow.
See, they're at work already, bringing in the wood.
Margery, suppose you go over and make sure that
they're building the fire properly, with plenty of
room for a good draught underneath"

"Who's going to take them in, and give them
their rings, Miss Eleanor?" asked Dolly. "You,
or Miss Turner?"

"Why, Miss Turner wants me to do it, Dolly,
because I'm older in the Camp Fire than she is.

She's given me the rings   I think it's quite exciting, really, taking so many new girls in all at
once.''

"Come on," cried Margery Burton, then.
"They're all ready and they want us to form the
procession now, and go over there."

"You are to light the fire, Margery. Are you
all ready?"

"Yes, indeed, Miss Eleanor. Shall I go ahead,
and start the flame?"

"Yes, do!"

Then while Margery disappeared, Eleanor, at
the head of the girls, started moving in the stately
Indian measure toward the dark pile of wood that
represented the fire that was so soon to blaze
up. As they walked they sang in low tones, so
that the melody rose and mingled with the waves
and the sighing of the wind.

Just as the first spark answered Margery's
efforts with her fire-making sticks, they reached
the fire, and sat down in a great circle, with a good
deal of space between each pair of girls. Eleanor

took her place in the centre, facing Margery, who now stood up, lifting a torch that she had lighted above her head. As she touched the tinder beneath the fire Eleanor raised her hand, and, as the flames began to crackle, she lowered it, and at once the girls began the song of Wo-he-lo:

> Wo-he-lo means love
> Wo-he-lo, wo-he-lo, wo-he-lo.
> We love love, for love is the heart of life.
> It is light and joy and sweetness,
> Comradeship and all dear kinship
> Love is the joy of service so deep
> That self is forgotten.
> Wo-he-lo means love.

Outside the circle now other and unseen voices joined them in the chorus:

> Wo-he-lo for aye,
> Wo-he-lo for aye,
> Wo-he-lo, wo-he-lo, wo-he-lo for aye!

Then for a moment utter silence, so that the murmur of the waves seemed amazingly loud. Then, their voices hushed, half the Manasquan girls chanted:

> Wo-he-lo for work!

And the others, their voices rising gradually, answered with:

Wo-he-lo for health!

And without a break in the rhythm, all the girls joined in the final

Wo-he-lo, wo-he-lo, wo-he-lo for love!

Then Margery, her torch still raised above her head, while she swung it slowly in time to the music of her song, sang alone:

O Fire!
Long years ago when our fathers fought with
   great animals you were their great protection
When they fought the cold of the cruel winter
   you saved them
When they needed food you changed the flesh
   of beasts into savory meat for them
During all the ages your mysterious flame has
   been a symbol to them for Spirit,
So, to-night, we light our fire in grateful re-
   membrance of the Great Spirit who gave you
   to us

Then Margery took her place in the circle, and Eleanor called the roll, giving each girl the name she had chosen as her fire name.

Then Mary Turner, in her new ceremonial robe, fringed with beads, slipped into the circle of the firelight, bright and vivid now.

"Oh, Wanaka," she said, calling Eleanor by her

ceremonial name, "I bring tonight these newcomers to the Camp Fire, to tell you their Desire, and to receive from you their rings "

One by one the girls of the Halsted Camp Fire stepped forward, and each repeated her Desire to be a Wood-Gatherer, and was received by Eleanor, who explained to each some new point of the Law of the Fire, so that all might learn. And to each, separately, as she slipped the silver ring of the Camp Fire on her finger, she repeated the beautiful exhortation:

> Firmly held by the sinews which bind them,
> As fagots are brought from the forest
> So cleave to these others, your sisters,
> Whenever, wherever you find them.
>
> Be strong as the fagots are sturdy;
> Be pure in your deepest desire;
> Be true to the truth that is in you;
> And—follow the law of the Fire!

One by one as they received their rings, the newcomers slipped into seats about the fire, each one finding a place between two of the Manasquan girls. Marcia Bates, flushed with pleasure, took a seat between Bessie and Dolly.

"Oh, how beautiful it all is!" she said. "I don't see how any of us could ever have laughed at the Camp Fire! But, of course, we didn't know about all this, or we never would have laughed as we did."

"I love the part about 'So cleave to these others, your sisters,'" said Dolly. "It's so fine to feel that wherever you go, you'll find friends wherever there's a Camp Fire—that you can show your ring, and be sure that there'll be someone who knows the same thing you know, and believes in the same sort of things!"

"Yes, that's lovely, Dolly. Of course, we've all read about this, but you have to do it to know how beautiful it is. I'm so glad you girls were here for this first Council Fire of ours You know how everything should be done, and that seems to make it so much better."

"It would have pleased you just as much, and been just as lovely if you'd done it all by yourselves, Marcia. It's the words, and the ceremony that are so beautiful—not the way we do it. Every

Camp Fire has its own way of doing things. For instance, some Camp Fires sing the Ode to Fire all together, but we have Margery do it alone because she has such a lovely voice ''

''I think it was splendid. I never had any idea she could sing so well.''

''Her voice is lovely, but it sounds particularly soft and true out in the open air this way, and without a piano to accompany her Mine doesn't —I'm all right to sing in a crowd, but when I try to sing by myself, it's just a sort of screech. There isn't any beauty to my tones at all, and I know it and don't try to sing alone.''

''Aren't they all in now?'' asked Bessie.

There had been a break in the steady appearance of new candidates before Eleanor. But, even as she spoke, another figure glided into the light.

''No. There's Gladys Cooper,'' said Marcia, with a little start.

''I wonder if she sees what there is to the Camp Fire now,'' said Dolly, speculatively.

''What is your desire?'' asked Eleanor.

"I desire to become a Camp Fire Girl and to obey the law of the Camp Fire," said Gladys, in a mechanical, sing-song voice, entirely different from the serious tones of those who had preceded her.

"She's laughing to herself," said Marcia, indignantly. "Just listen! She's repeating the Desire as if it were a bit of doggerel"

They heard her saying:

"Seek beauty, Give service, Pursue knowledge, Hold on to health, Glorify work, Be happy. This law of the Camp Fire I will strive to follow."

"Give service," repeated Eleanor slowly. "You have heard what I said to the other girls, Gladys. I want you to understand this point of the law. It is the most important of all, perhaps. It means that you must be friendly to your sisters of the Camp Fire; that you must love them, and put them above yourself"

"I must do all that for my chums—the girls in our Camp Fire, you mean, I suppose?" said Gladys. "I don't care anything about these other girls. And, Miss Mercer, all that you're going to say in a minute—'So cleave to these others, your sisters'—that doesn't mean the girls in any old Camp Fire, does it?''

Startled, Eleanor was silent for a moment. Mary Turner looked at Gladys indignantly.

"It means every girl in every Camp Fire," said Eleanor, finally. "And more than that, you must serve others, in or out of the Camp Fire."

"Oh, that's nonsense!" said Gladys. "I couldn't do that "

"Then you are not fit to receive your ring," said Eleanor.

CHAPTER VI

There was a gasp of astonishment and dismay
from the girls. Somehow all seemed to feel as
if Eleanor's reproach were directed at them instead of at the pale and angry Gladys, who stood,
scarcely able to believe her ears, looking at the
Guardian There had been no anger in Eleanor's
voice—only sorrow and distress.

"Why, what do you mean, Miss Mercer?"
Gladys gasped.

"Exactly what I say, Gladys," said Eleanor,
in the same level voice. "You are not fit to be
one of us unless you mean sincerely and earnestly
to keep the Law of the Fire. We are a sister-
hood; no girl who is not only willing, but eager,
to become our sister, may join us "

Slowly the meaning of her rejection seemed to
sink into the mind of Gladys.

91

"Do you mean that you're not going to let me join?" she asked in a shrill, high-pitched voice that showed she was on the verge of giving way to an outbreak of hysterical anger

"For your own sake it is better that you should not join now, Gladys. Listen to me. I do not blame you greatly for this. I would rather have you act this way than be a hypocrite, pretending to believe in our law when you do not."

"Oh, I hate you! I hate the Camp Fire! I wouldn't join for anything in the world, after this!"

"There will be time to settle that when we are ready to let you join, Gladys," said Eleanor, a little sternness creeping into her voice, as if she were growing angry for the first time. " To join the Camp Fire is a privilege. Remember this— no girl does the Camp Fire a favor by joining it. The Camp Fire does not need any one girl, no matter how clever, or how pretty, or how able she may be, as much as that girl needs the Camp

Fire. The Camp Fire, as a whole, is a much greater, finer thing than any single member."

Sobs of anger were choking Gladys when she tried to answer. She could not form intelligible words

Eleanor glanced at Mary Turner, and the Guardian of the new Camp Fire, on the hint, put her arm about Gladys

"I think you'd better go back to the camp now, dear," she said, very gently. "You and I will have a talk presently, when you feel better, and perhaps you will see that you are wrong "

All the life and spirit seemed to have left the girls as Gladys, her head bowed, the sound of her sobs still plainly to be heard, left the circle of the firelight and made her lonely way over the beach toward the tents of her own camp For a few moments silence reigned Then Eleanor spoke, coolly and steadily, although Mary Turner, who was close to her, knew what an effort her seeming calm represented.

"We have had a hard thing to do to-night,"

she said. "I know that none of you will add to what Gladys has made herself suffer. She is in the wrong, but I think that very few of us will have any difficulty in remembering many times when we have been wrong, and have been sure that we were right Gladys thinks now that we are all against her—that we wanted to humiliate her. We must make her understand that she is wrong. Remember, Wo-he-lo means love."

She paused for a moment.

"Wo-he-lo means love," she repeated. "And not love for those whom we cannot help loving. The love that is worth while is that we give to those who repel us, who do not want our love. It is easy to love those who love us. But in time we can make Gladys love us by showing that we want to love her and do what we can to make her happy And now, since I think none of us feel like staying here, we will sing our good-night song and disperse."

And the soft voices rose like a benediction, mingling in the lovely strains of that most beautiful of all the Camp Fire songs.

Silently, and without the usual glad talk that followed the ending of a Council Fire, the circle broke up, and the girls, in twos and threes, spread over the beach

"Walk over with me, won't you?" Marcia Bates begged Dolly and Bessie. "Oh, I'm so ashamed! I never thought Gladys would act like that!"

"It isn't your fault, Marcia," said Dolly. "Don't be silly about it. And, do you know, I'm not angry a bit! Just at first I thought I was going to be furious. But—well, somehow I can't help admiring Gladys! I like her better than I ever did before, I really do believe!"

"Oh, I do!" said Bessie, her eyes glowing. "Wasn't she splendid? Of course, she's all wrong, but she had to be plucky to stand up there like that, when she knew everyone was against her!"

"But she had no right to insult all you girls, Bessie."

"I don't believe she meant to insult us a bit," said Dolly. "I don't think she thought much about us. It's just that she has always been brought up to feel a certain way about things, and she couldn't change all at once. A whole lot of girls, while they believed just what she did, and hated the whole idea just as much, would never have dared to say so, when they knew no one agreed with them."

"Yes, it's just as Miss Eleanor said," said Bessie. "She's not a hypocrite, no matter what her other faults are She's not afraid to say just what she thinks—and that's pretty fine, after all "

"I wish she could hear you," said Marcia, indignantly. "Oh, it's splendid of you, but I can't feel that way, and there's no use pretending. I suppose the real reason I'm so angry is that I'm really very fond of Gladys, and I hate to see her acting this way. She's making a perfect fool of herself, I think."

"But just think of how splendid it will be when

she sees she is wrong, Marcia," said Bessie "Because you want to remember if she's plucky enough to hold out against all her friends this way she will be plucky enough to own up when she sees the truth, too."

"Yes, and she'll be a convert worth making, too," said Dolly. "There's just one thing I'm thinking of, Marcia. Will she stay here? Don't you suppose she'll go home right away? I know I would I wouldn't want to stay around this beach after what happened at the Council Fire to-night"

They never heard Marcia's answer to that question, for in the darkness, Gladys herself, shaking with anger, rose and confronted them.

"You bet I'm going to stay!" she declared, furiously. "And I'll get even with you, Dolly Ransom, and your nasty old Miss Mercer, and the whole crew of you! Maybe you've been able to set all my friends against me—I'm glad of it!"

"No one is set against you, Gladys," said Marcia, gently.

6—C7

"Maybe you don't call it that, Marcia Bates, but I've got my own opinion of a lot of girls who call themselves my friends and side against me the way you've done!"

"Why, Gladys, I haven't done a thing—"

"That's just it, you sneak! Why, do you suppose I'd have let them treat you as I was treated to-night? If it had happened to you and I'd joined before, I'd have got up and thrown their nasty old ring back at them! I don't want their old ring! I've got much prettier ones of my own —gold, and set with sapphires and diamonds!"

"I'm very glad you're going to stay, Gladys!" said Dolly. "I'm sorry I've been cross when I spoke to you lately two or three times, and I hope you'll forgive me. And I think you'll see soon that we're not at all what you think we are in the Camp Fire "

"Oh, you needn't talk that way to me, Dolly Ransom! You can pretend all you like to be a saint, but I've known you too long to swallow all that! You've done just as many mean things as

anyone else! And now you stand around and act
as if you were ashamed to know me. Just you
wait! I'll get even with you, and all the rest of
your new friends, if it's the last thing I ever do!''

Bessie's hand reached out for Dolly's She
knew her chum well enough to understand that if
Dolly controlled her temper now it would only be
by the exercise of the grimmest determination.
Sure enough, Dolly's hand was trembling, and
Bessie could almost feel the hot anger that was
swelling up in her. But Dolly mastered herself
nobly.

''You can't make me angry now, Gladys,'' said
Dolly, finally ''You're perfectly right; I've done
things that are meaner than anything you did at
Lake Dean. And I'm just as sorry for them now
as you will be when you understand better ''

''Well, you needn't preach to me!'' said Gladys,
fiercely. ''And you can give up expecting me to
run away. I'm not a coward, whatever else I may
be! And I'd never be able to hold up my head
if I thought a lot of common girls had frightened

me into running away from this place. I'm going
to stay here, and I'm going to have a good time,
and you'd better look out for yourselves—that's
all I can say! Maybe I know more about you
than you think.''

And then she turned on her heel and left
them

"Whew!'' said Marcia "I don't see how you
kept your temper, Dolly. If she'd said half as
much to me as she did to you, I never could have
stood it, I can tell you! Whatever did she mean
by what she said just then about knowing more
than we thought?''

"I don't know,'' said Dolly, rather anxiously.
"But look here, Marcia, I might as well tell you
now There's likely to be a good deal of excitement here.''

"Yes,'' said Bessie, rather bitterly. "And it's
all my fault—mine and Zara's. that is ''

"I don't see what you can mean,'' said Marcia,
mystified

"Well, it's quite a long story, but I really think

you'd better know all about it, Marcia," said Dolly.

And so, with occasional help from Bessie herself, when Dolly forgot something, or when Bessie's ideas disagreed with hers, Dolly poured the story of the adventures of Bessie and Zara since their flight from Hedgeville into Marcia's ears

"Why, I never heard of such a thing!" Marcia exclaimed, when the story was told. "So that fire last night wasn't an accident at all?"

" We're quite sure it wasn't, Marcia. And don't you think it looks as if we were right?"

"It certainly does, and I think it's dreadful, Dolly—just dreadful. Oh, Bessie, I am so sorry for you!"

She threw her arms about Bessie impulsively and kissed her, while Dolly, delighted, looked on.

"Doesn't it make you love her more than ever?" she said. "And Bessie is so foolish about it sometimes. She seems to think that girls won't want to have anything to do with her, because she hasn't had a home and parents like the rest of us—or like most of us."

"That *is* awfully silly, Bessie," said Marcia. "As if it was your fault! People are going to like you for what you are, and for the way you behave—not on account of things that you really haven't a thing to do with Sensible people, I mean. Of course, if they're like Gladys—but then most people aren't, I think."

"Of course they're not!" said Dolly, stoutly. "And, besides, I'm just sure that Bessie is going to find out about her father and mother some day. I don't believe Mr Holmes would be taking all the trouble he has about her unless there were something very surprising about her history that we don't know anything about. Do you, Marcia?"

"Of course not! He's got something up his sleeve. Probably she is heiress to a fortune, or something like that, and he wants to get hold of it. He's a very rich man, isn't he, Dolly?"

"Yes. You know he's the owner of a great big department store at home. And Bessie says

that it can't be any question of money that makes
him so anxious to get hold of her and of Zara,
because he has so much already.''

"H'm! I guess people who have money like
to make more, Dolly. I've heard my father talk
about that. He says they're never content, and
that's one reason why so many men work themselves to death, simply because they haven't got
sense enough to stop and rest when they have
enough money to live comfortably for the rest of
their lives ''

"That's another thing I've told her. And she
says that can't be the reason, but just the same
she never suggests a better one to take its place.''

"Look here," said Marcia, thoughtfully. "If
Mr. Holmes is spending so much money, doesn't
it cost a whole lot to stop him from doing what
he's trying to do, whatever that is? I'm just
thinking—my father has ever so much, you know,
and I know if I told him, he'd be glad to spend
whatever was needed—''

Bessie finished unhappily.

"Oh, that's one thing that is worrying me terribly'" she cried "I just know that Miss Eleanor and Mr. Jamieson must have spent a terrible lot on my affairs already, and I don't see how I'm ever going to pay them back' And if I ever mention it, Miss Eleanor gets almost angry, and says I mustn't talk about it at all, even think of it "

"Why, of course you mustn't. It would be awful to think that those horrid people were able to get hold of you and make you unhappy just because they had money and you didn't, Bessie "

And Dolly echoed her exclamation Naturally enough, Marcia, whose parents were among the richest people in the state, thought little of money, and Dolly, who had always had plenty, even though her family was by no means as rich as Marcia's, felt the same way about the matter. Neither of them valued money particularly; but Bessie, because she had lived ever since she could remember in a family where the pinch of actual poverty was always felt, had a much truer appreciation of the value of money.

She did not want to possess money, but she had a good deal of native pride, and it worried her constantly to think that her good friends were spending money that she could see no prospect, however remote, of repaying.

"I wish there was some way to keep me from having to take all the money they spend on me," she said, wistfully "As soon as we get back to the city, I'm going to find some work to do, so that I can support myself."

She half expected Marcia to assail that idea, for it seemed to her that, nice as she was, she belonged, like Gladys Cooper, to the class that looked down on work and workers. But to her surprise, Marcia gave a cry of admiration.

"It's splendid for you to feel that way, Bessie!" she said. "But, just the same, I believe you'll have to wait until things are more settled. It would be so much easier for Mr. Holmes to get hold of you if you were working, you know."

"She's going to come and stay with me just as long as she wants to," said Dolly. "And, anyhow, I really believe things are going to be settled for her. Perhaps I've heard something, too!"

CHAPTER VII

THE CHALLENGE

When Bessie and Dolly returned to their own camp they found Eleanor Mercer waiting for them, and as soon as she was alone with them, she did something that, for her, was very rare. She asked them about their talk with Marcia Bates.

"You know that as a rule I don't interfere," she said. "Unless there is something that makes it positively necessary for me to intrude myself, I leave you to yourselves."

"Why, we would have told you all about it, anyhow, Miss Eleanor," said Dolly, surprised.

"Yes, but even so, I want you to know that I'm sorry to feel that I should ask you to tell me. As a rule, I would rather let you girls work all these things out by yourselves, even if I see very plainly that you are making mistakes. I think you can sometimes learn more by doing a thing wrong, provided that you are following your own ideas, than by doing it right when you are simply doing what someone else tells you.''

''I see what you mean, Miss Eleanor,'' said Bessie. ''But this time we really haven't done anything. We saw Gladys, too, and—''

She went on to tell of their talk with Marcia and of the unpleasant episode created by Gladys when she had overheard them talking.

''I think you've done very well indeed,'' said Eleanor, with a sigh of relief, when she had heard the story. ''I was so afraid that you would lose your temper, Dolly. Not that I could really have blamed you if you had, but, oh, it's so much better that you didn't. So Gladys has decided to stay, has she?''

''Yes,'' said Dolly. ''But Marcia seemed to think Miss Turner might make her go home.''

''She won't,'' said Eleanor. ''She was thinking of it, but I have had a talk with her, and we both decided that that wouldn't do much good. It might save us some trouble, but it wouldn't do

Gladys any good, and, after all, she's the one we've got to consider "

Dolly didn't say anything, but it was plain from her look that she did not understand

"What I mean is," Eleanor went on, "that there's a chance here for us to make a real convert—one who will count. It's easy enough to make girls understand our Camp Fire idea when they want to like it, and feel sure that they're going to. The hard cases are the girls like Gladys, who have a prejudice against the Camp Fire without really knowing anything at all about it. And if the Camp Fire idea is the fine, strong, splendid thing we all believe, why, this is a good time to prove it. If it is, Gladys won't be able to hold out against it."

"That's what I've thought from the first, Miss Eleanor," said Bessie. "And I'm sure she will like us better presently."

"Well, if she is willing to stay, she is to stay," said Eleanor. "And she is to be allowed to do everything the other girls do, except, of course, she can't actually take part in a Council Fire until she's a member. We don't want her to feel that she is being punished, and Miss Turner is going to try to make her girls treat her just as if nothing had happened. That's what I want our Manasquan girls to do, too."

"They will, then, if I've got anything to say," declared Dolly, vehemently. "And I guess I've got more reason to be down on her than any of the others except Bessie. So if I'm willing to be nice to her, I certainly don't see why the others should hesitate."

"Remember this, Dolly. You're willing to be nice to her now, but she may make it pretty hard. You're going to have a stiff test of your self-control and your temper for the next few days. When people are in the wrong and know it, but aren't ready to admit it and be sorry, they usually go out of their way to be nasty to those they have injured—"

"Oh, I don't care what she says or does now," said Dolly. "If I could talk to her to-night with-

out getting angry, I think I'm safe   I never came
so near to losing my temper without really doing
it in my whole life before.''

"Well, that's fine, Dolly. Keep it up. Remember this is pretty hard for poor Miss Turner.
Here she is, just starting in as a Camp Fire
Guardian, and at the very beginning she has this
trouble! But if she does make Gladys come
around, it will be a great victory for her, and I
want you and all of our girls to do everything
you can to help.''

Then with a hearty good-night she turned away,
and it was plain that she was greatly relieved by
what Bessie and Dolly had told her.

"Well, I don't know what you're going to do,
Bessie,'' said Dolly, ''but I'm going to turn in
and sleep! I'm just beginning to realize how tired
I am.''

"I'm tired, too. We've really had enough to
make us pretty tired, haven't we?''

And this time they were able to sleep through
the whole night without interruption. The peace

and calm of Plum Beach were disturbed by
nothing more noisy than gentle waves, and
the whole camp awoke in the morning vastly re-
freshed

The sun shone down gloriously, and the cloud-
less sky proclaimed that it was to be a day fit for
any form of sport   A gentle breeze blew in from
the sea, dying away to nothing sometimes, and
the water inside the sand bar was so smooth and
inviting that half a dozen of the girls, with Dolly
at their head, scampered in for a plunge before
breakfast.

"They're swimming over at the other camp,
too," cried Dolly   "See?   Oh, I bet we'll have
some good times with them.   We ought to be able
to have all sorts of fun in the water "

"Aren't there any boats here beside that old
flat bottom skiff?" asked Bessie.

"Aren't there?   Just wait till you see!   If we
hadn't had all that excitement yesterday Captain
Salters would have brought the *Eleanor* over.   He
will to-day, too, and then you'll see."

"What will I see, Dolly? Remember I haven't been here before, like you "

"Oh, she's the dandiest little boat, Bessie—a little sloop, and as fast as a steamboat, if she's handled right "

"Now we'll never hear the end of her," said Margery Burton, with a comical gesture of despair. "You've touched the button, Bessie, and Dolly will keep on telling us about the *Eleanor,* and how fast she is, until someone sits on her!"

"You're jealous, Margery," laughed Dolly, in high good humor. "Margery's pretty clever, Bessie, and when it comes to cooking—my!" She smacked her lips loudly, as if to express her sense of how well Margery could cook. "But she can't sail a boat !"

"Here's Captain Salters now—and he's towing the *Eleanor,* all right, Dolly," cried one of the other girls.

"Oh, I'm so glad!" cried Dolly. "Bessie, you've never been in a sail boat, have you? I'll have to show you how everything is done, and

6—C8

then we'll have some bully fine times together. You'll love it, I know.''

''She won't if she's inclined to be seasick,'' said Margery. ''The trouble with Dolly is that she can never have enough of a good thing. The higher the wind, the happier Dolly is. She'll keep on until the boat heels away over, and until you think you're going over the next minute—and she calls that having a good time!''

''Well, I never heard you begging me to quit, Margery Burton!'' said Dolly. ''You're an old fraud—that's what you are! You pretend you are terribly frightened, and all the time you're enjoying it just as much as I am. I wish there was some way we could have a race. That's where the real fun comes in with a sail boat.''

''You could get all the racing you want over at Bay City, Dolly The yacht club there has races every week, I think ''

''But Miss Eleanor would never let me sail in one of those races, Margery. I guess she's right, too. I may be pretty good for a girl, but I'm afraid I wouldn't have a chance with those men.''

Margery pretended to faint.

''Listen to that, will you?'' she exclaimed. ''Here's Dolly actually saying that someone might be able to do something better than she could! I'll believe in almost anything after that!''

''Well, you can laugh all you like,'' said Dolly, with spirit '' But if we should have a race, I'll be captain, and I know some people who won't get a chance to be even on the crew. They'll feel pretty sorry they were so fresh, I guess, when they have to stay ashore cooking dinner while I and my crew are out in the sloop!''

Then from the beach came the primitive call to breakfast—made by the simple process of pounding very hard on the bottom of a frying pan with a big tin spoon. That ended the talk about Dolly's qualifications as a yacht captain, and there was a wild rush to the beach, and to the tents, since those who had been in for an early swim could not sit down to breakfast in their wet bathing

suits   But no one took any great length of time
to dress, since here the utmost simplicity ruled in
clothes

"Well, what's the programme for to-day,
girls?" asked Eleanor, after the meal was over.

"Each for herself!" cried half a dozen voices.
And a broken chorus rose in agreement.

"I want to fish!" cried one

"A long walk for me!" cried another.

"I'd like to make up a party to go over to
Bay City and buy things   We haven't been near
a store for weeks!" suggested another.

"All right," said Eleanor   "Everyone can do
exactly what she likes between the time we finish
clearing up after lunch and dinner. I think we'll
have the same rule we did at Long Lake—four
girls attend to the camp work each day, while
the other eight do as they like. You can draw
lots or arrange it among yourselves, I don't
care."

"Yes, that's a fine arrangement," said Dolly.
"It's a little harder for the four who work than

it would be if we all pitched in, but no one really
has to work any harder, for all that.''

"It's even in the long run," said Eleanor.
"And it gives some of you a chance to do things
that call for a whole afternoon. All agreed to
that, are you?''

It was Eleanor's habit, whenever possible, to
submit such minor details of camp life to a vote
of the girls. Her authority, of course. was complete. If she gave an order, it had to be obeyed,
and she had the right, if she decided it was best,
to send any or all of the girls home. But—and
many guardians find it a good plan—she preferred
to give the girls a good deal of latitude and real
independence.

One result was that, whenever she did give a
positive order, it was obeyed unquestioningly.
The girls knew by experience that usually she was
content to suggest things, and even agree to
methods that she herself would not have chosen,
and, as they were not accustomed to receiving
positive orders on all sorts of subjects, they under-

stood without being told that there was a good
reason for those that were issued. Another result,
of course, and the most important, was that the
girls, growing used to governing themselves, grew
more self-reliant, and better fitted to cope with
emergencies.

The girls were still washing the breakfast dishes
when Marcia Bates walked along the beach and
was greeted with a merry hail by Dolly and the
others.

"I'm here as an ambassador or something like
that," she announced. "That little sloop out there
is yours, isn't she?"

"Well, we'll have ours here as soon as
it's towed over from Bay City. And we want
to challenge you to a regular yacht race. I
asked Miss Turner if we might, and she said
yes."

"I think that would be fine sport," said Eleanor.
"Dolly Ransom is skipper of our sloop. Suppose
you talk it over with her."

"I think it would be fine, Marcia!" said Dolly.

with shining eyes. "I was just wishing for a race this morning. When shall we have it?"

"Why not this afternoon?" asked Marcia. "We could race out to the lighthouse on the rock out there and back. That's not very far, but it's far enough to make a good race, I should think."

"Splendid!" said Dolly. "What sort of a boat is yours?"

"Just the same as yours, I think. We can see when they come, and if one is bigger than the other, we can arrange about a handicap. Miss Turner said she thought she ought to be in one boat, and Miss Mercer in the other."

"Yes, I think so, too. And I'll be skipper of our boat, and have Bessie King and Margery Burton for a crew. Who is your skipper?"

"Gladys Cooper," answered Marcia, after a slight pause.

"Bully for her! Just you tell her I'm going to beat her so badly she won't even know she's in a race."

Marcia laughed.

"All right," she said. "I'll let you know when we're ready"

"Now, then, Bessie," said Dolly, "just you come out with me to the sloop in that skiff, and I'll show you just what you'll have to do. It won't be hard—you'll only have to obey orders. But you'd better know the names of the ropes, so that you'll understand my orders when 1 give them"

So for an hour Bessie, delighted with the appearance of the trim little sloop, took lessons from Dolly in the art of handling small sailing craft.

"You'll get along all right," said Dolly, as they pulled back to the beach. "Don't get excited. That's the only thing to remember. We'll wear our bathing suits, of course, so that if we get spilled into the water, there'll be no harm done."

"We've got a good chance of being spilled, too," said Margery. "I know how Dolly likes to sail a boat. So if you don't want a ducking, you'd better make her take someone else in your place."

"I wouldn't miss it for anything," said Bessie, happily. "I've never even seen a yacht race. I bet it must be lots of fun."

"It won't be rough, anyhow," said Eleanor, after they had landed. She looked out to sea. "It's pretty hazy out there, Dolly. Think there'll be enough wind?"

"Oh, yes," said Dolly. "Plenty! It won't be stiff, of course, and we won't make good time, but that doesn't make any difference It's as good for them as for us—and the other way round."

CHAPTER VIII

The sloop that was to represent the Halsted Camp Fire in the race arrived in the cove late in the morning, and from the shore there seemed to be no difference in size between the two little craft. They were different, and one might prove swifter than the other, for no two boats of that sort were ever exactly alike. But so far as could be judged, the race was likely to be a test rather of how the boats were sailed than of their speed, boat for boat.

"I think you can sail on even terms, Dolly," said Eleanor. "I don't believe there'll be any need for either of you to give away any time to the other."

"I'm glad of that, Miss Eleanor," said Dolly. "It seems much nicer when you're exactly even at the start."

123

"Here's Miss Turner now," said Bessie. "I guess they must be about ready to start I hope I'll do the right thing when you tell me, Dolly, but I'm dreadfully afraid I won't."

"Don't worry about it, and you'll be much more likely to get along well," said Margery Burton, calmly. "And remember that this race isn't the most important thing in the world, even if Dolly thinks it is "

"Oh, it's all right for you to talk that way now," said Dolly. "But wait till we're racing, Bessie. You'll find she's just as much worked up about it then as I am—and probably more so."

"Well, all ready, Nell?" asked Mary Turner, coming up to them then. "Gladys seems to think she's about ready to start, so I thought I'd walk over and arrange about the details."

"I think the best way to fix up the start will be for the two sloops to reach the opening in the bar together," said Eleanor. "They can start there and finish there, you see, and that will save the need of having someone to take the time. We really haven't anyone who can do that properly. If we're close together at the start you and I can call to one another and agree upon the moment when the race has actually begun.''

''All right,'' said Miss Turner. ''I'd thought of that myself.'' She lowered her voice ''I didn't like to oppose this race, Nell,'' she said, speaking so that only Eleanor could hear her, ''but I'm not at all sure that it's going to be a good thing ''

''Why not? I thought it would be good sport ''

''It ought to be, but I don't know how good a sportsman Gladys is If she wins, it will probably make her feel a lot better. But if she loses—!''

''I hadn't thought of that side of it,'' said Eleanor. ''But—oh, well, even so, I think it will probably be a good thing. Gladys has got a lot of hard lessons to learn, and if this is one of them, the sooner she learns it, the better You and I will be along to see fair play. That will keep her from having anything to say if she does lose, you see ''

"We're in for it, anyhow, so I didn't mean to have you worry about it. I think anything that I might have done to stop the race would have done more harm than the race itself can possibly do, in any case.''

"I'm quite sure of that, Mary. Well, we'll get aboard our yacht and you'd better do the same. They're probably waiting impatiently for you.''

The flat-bottomed skiff that Bessie had despised proved handy for carrying the *Eleanor's* crew out to her. While the others climbed aboard, Dolly, who insisted upon attending to everything herself when she possibly could, arranged a floating anchor that would keep the boat in place against their return, and a few moments later the *Eleanor's* snowy sails rose, flapping idly in the faint breeze.

"Get up that anchor!" directed Dolly. "Bessie, you help Margery. She'll show you what to do.''

Then a shiver shook the little craft, the wind filled the sails, and in a few moments they were

creeping slowly toward the opening in the bar
Seated at the helm, Dolly looked over toward the
other camp and saw that the other yacht was also
under way.

"What do they call their boat?" she asked.

"The *Defiance*," said Eleanor.

Dolly laughed at the answer.

"I bet I know who named her!" she said,
merrily. "If that isn't just like Gladys Cooper!
Well, I want a good race, and I can have just as
much fun if we're beaten, as long as I can feel
that I haven't made any mistakes in sailing the
Eleanor. But—well, I guess I would like to beat
Gladys. I bet she's awfully sure of winning!"

"She's had more experience in sailing boats
like these than you have, Dolly," said Eleanor.

"She's welcome to it," said Dolly. "I shan't
make any excuses if I lose. I'll be ready to admit
that she's better than I am."

The two boats converged together upon the
opening in the bar, and soon those on one could
see everything aboard the other. Gladys Cooper,

like Dolly, sat at the helm, steering her boat, and
a look of grim determination was in her eyes and
on her unsmiling face.

"She certainly does want to win," said Margery "She's taking this too seriously—score one
for Dolly."

"You think she'd do better if she weren't so
worked up, Margery?"

"Of course she would! There are just two
ways to take a race or a sporting contest of any
sort—as a game or as a bit of serious work. If
you do the very best you can and forget about
winning, you'll win a good deal oftener than you
lose, if your best is any good at all. It's that way
in football I've heard boys say that when they
have played against certain teams, they've known
right after the start that they were going to win,
because the other team's players would lose
their tempers the first time anything went
wrong "

"We seem to be on even terms now," said
Eleanor, and, cupping her hands, she hailed Mary

Turner. "All right? We might as well call this a start "

"All right," said Mary. "Shall I give the word?"

"Go ahead!" said Eleanor.

Instantly Dolly, with a quick look at her sails, which were hanging limp again, since she had altered the course a trifle, became all attention.

"One—two—three—go!" called Miss Turner, clapping her hands at the word "go."

And instantly Dolly shifted her helm once more, so that the wind filled the sails, and the *Eleanor* shot for the opening in the bar. Quick as she had been, however, she was no quicker than Gladys, and the *Defiance* and the *Eleanor* passed through the bar and out into the open sea together. Here there was more motion, since the short, choppy waves outside the bar were never wholly still, no matter how calm the sea might seem to be. But Bessie, who had been rather nervous as to the effect of this motion, which she had been warned to dread, found it by no means unpleasant.

6—C9

For a few moments Dolly's orders flew sharply. Although the wind was very light, there was enough of it to give fair speed, and the sails had to be trimmed to get the utmost possible out of it while it lasted. Both boats tacked to starboard, sailing along a slanting line that seemed likely to carry them far to one side of the lighthouse that was their destination, and Bessie wondered at this.

"We're not sailing straight for the lighthouse," she said. "Isn't that supposed to be where we turn? Don't we have to sail around it?"

"Yes, but we can't go straight there, because the wind isn't right," explained Dolly. "We'll keep on this way for a spell; then we'll come about and tack to port, and then to starboard again. In that way we can beat the wind, you see, and make it work for us, even if it doesn't want to."

Half way to the lighthouse there was less than a hundred feet between the boats. The *Defiance* seemed to be a little ahead, but the advantage, if she really had one at all, was not enough to have any real effect on the race.

"Going out isn't going to give either of us much chance to gain, I guess," said Dolly. "The real race will be when we're going back, with what wind there is behind us."

But soon it seemed that Dolly had made a rash prediction, for when she came about and started to beat up to port, the *Defiance* held to her course.

"Well, she can do that if she wants to," said Dolly. "Just the same, I think she's going too far "

"It looks to me as if she were pretty sure of what she's doing, though, Dolly," said Margery, anxiously "Don't you think you tacked a little too soon?"

"If I thought that I wouldn't have done it, Margery," said Dolly. "Don't bother me with silly questions now; I've got to figure on tacking again so as to make that turn with the least possible waste of time."

"Don't talk to the 'man' at the wheel," advised Eleanor, with a laugh. "She's irritable."

A good many of the nautical terms used so free-

ly by the others might have been so much Greek
for all Bessie could understand of them, but the
race itself had awakened her interest and now
held it as scarcely anything she had ever done
had been able to do.

She kept her eyes fixed on the other boat, and
at last she gave a cry.

"Look! They're going to turn now."

"Score one for Gladys, Margery," said Dolly,
quietly. "She's certainly stolen a march on me.
Do you see that? She's going to make her turn
on the next tack, and I believe she'll gain nearly
five minutes on us. That was clever, and it was
good work."

"Never mind, Dolly," said Margery. "You've
still got a chance to catch her going home before
the wind. I know how fast the *Eleanor* is at that
sort of work. If the *Defiance* is any better, she
ought to be racing for some real cups."

"Oh, don't try to cheer me up! I made an awful mess of that, Margery, and I know it. Gladys
had more nerve than I, that's all. She deserves

the lead she's got It isn't a question of the boats, at all. The *Defiance* is being sailed better than the *Eleanor.*"

"Margery's right, though, Dolly," said Eleanor. "The race isn't over yet. You haven't given up hope, have you?"

"Given up?" cried Dolly, scornfully, through set teeth. "Just you watch, that's all! I'm going to get home ahead if I have to swamp us all."

"That's more like her," Margery whispered to Bessie.

And now even Bessie could see that the *Defiance* had gained a big advantage. Before her eyes, not so well trained as those of the others to weigh every consideration in such a contest, had not seen what was really happening. But it was plain enough now. Even while the *Defiance* was holding on for the lighthouse, on a straight course, the *Eleanor* had to come about and start beating up toward it, and the *Defiance* made the turn, and, with spannaker set, was skimming gaily for home a full five minutes before the *Eleanor* circled the lighthouse.

In fact, the *Defiance,* homeward bound, passed them, and Mary Turner laughed gaily as she hailed Eleanor.

"This is pretty bad," she called "Better luck next time, Nell!'"

Marcia Bates waved her hand gaily to them, but Gladys Cooper, her eyes straight ahead, her hand on the tiller, paid no attention to them. There was no mistaking the look of triumph on her face, however. She was sure she was going to win, and she was glorying in her victory already.

"I'll make her smile on the other side of her face yet," said Dolly, viciously. "She might have waved her hand, at least. If we're good enough to race with, we're good enough for her to be decently polite to us, I should think."

"Easy, Dolly!" said Margery. "It won't help any for you to lose your temper, you know. Remember you've still got to sail your boat."

The *Defiance* was far ahead when, at last, after a wait that seemed to those on board interminable, the *Eleanor* rounded the lighthouse in her turn.

"Lively now!" commanded Dolly. "Shake out the spannaker! We're going to need all the sail we've got There isn't enough wind now to make a flag stand out properly."

"And they got the best of it, too," lamented Margery. "You see, Bessie, the good wind there was when they started back carried them well along We won't get that, and we'll keep falling further and further behind, because they've probably still got more wind than we have. It'll die out here before it does where they are."

Dolly stood up now, and cast her eyes behind her on the horizon, and all about And suddenly, without warning, she put the helm over, and the *Eleanor* stood off to port, heading, as it seemed, far from the opening in the bar that was the finishing line.

"Dolly, are you crazy?" exclaimed Margery. "This is a straight run before the wind!"

"Suppose there isn't any wind?" asked Dolly. The strained, anxious look had left her eyes, and she seemed calm now, almost elated. "Margery, you're a fine cook, but you've got a lot to learn yet about sailing a boat!"

Bessie was completely mystified, and a look at Margery showed her that she, too, although silenced, was far from being satisfied. But now Margery suddenly looked off on the surface of the water, and gave a glad cry.

"Oh, fine, Dolly!" she exclaimed. "I see what you're up to—and I bet Gladys thinks you're perfectly insane, too!"

"She'll soon know I'm not," said Dolly, grimly. "I only hope she doesn't know enough to do the same thing. I don't see how she can miss, though, unless she can't see in time."

Still Bessie was mystified, and she did not like to ask for an explanation, especially since she felt certain that one would be forthcoming anyhow in a few moments. And, sure enough, it was. For suddenly she felt a breath of wind, and, at the

same instant Dolly brought the *Eleanor* up before
the wind again, and for the first time Bessie understood what the little sloop's real speed was.

"You see, Bessie," said Margery, "Dolly knew
that the wind was dying. It's a puffy, uncertain
sort of wind, and very often, on a day like this,
there'll be plenty of breeze in one spot, and none
at all in another."

"Oh, so we came over here to find this breeze!"
said Bessie.

"Yes. It was the only chance. If we had stayed
on the other course we might have found enough
breeze to carry us home, but we would have gone
at a snail's pace, just as we were doing, and there
was no chance at all to catch Gladys and the *Defiance* that way."

"We haven't caught them yet, you know," said
Dolly.

"But we're catching them," said Bessie, exult-
ingly. "Even I can see that. Look! They're
just crawling along."

"Still, even at the rate they're going, ten minutes more will bring them to the finish," said Margery, anxiously. "Do you think she can make it, Dolly?"

"I don't know," said Dolly "I've done all I can, anyhow. There isn't a thing to do now but hold her steady and trust to this shift of the wind to last long enough to carry us home "

Now the *Eleanor* was catching the *Defiance* fast, and nearing her more and more rapidly. It was a strange and mysterious thing to Bessie to see that of two yachts so close together—there was less than a quarter of a mile between them now—one could have her sails filled with a good breeze while the other seemed to have none at all. But it was so. The *Defiance* was barely moving; she seemed as far from the finish now as she had been when Margery spoke.

"They're stuck—they're becalmed," said Margery, finally, when five minutes of steady gazing hadn't shown the slightest apparent advance by the *Defiance*. "Oh, Dolly, we're going to beat them!"

"I guess we are," said Dolly, with a sigh of satisfaction. "It was about the most hopeless looking race I ever saw twenty minutes ago, but you never can tell"

And now every minute seemed to make the issue more and more certain Sometimes a little puff of wind would strike the *Defiance,* fill her sails, and push her a little nearer her goal, but the hopes that those puffs must have raised in Dolly's rival and her crew were false, for each died away before the *Defiance* really got moving again.

And at last, passing within a hundred yards, so that they could see poor Gladys, her eyes filled with tears, the *Eleanor* slipped by the *Defiance* and took the lead And then, by some strange irony of fate, the wind came to the *Defiance*—but it came too late. For the *Eleanor,* slipping through the water as if some invisible force had been dragging her, passed through the opening and into the still waters of the cove fully two hundred feet in the lead.

"That certainly was **your** victory, Dolly," said

Eleanor. "If you hadn't found that wind, we'd still be floundering around somewhere near the lighthouse."

"I do feel sorry for Gladys, though," said Dolly. "It must have been hard—when she was so sure that she had won."

CHAPTER IX

"That was bad luck. You really deserved to win that race, Gladys," Dolly called out, as the *Defiance* came within hailing distance of the *Eleanor* again.

Gladys looked at her old friend but said not a word. It was very plain that the loss of the race, which she had considered already won, was a severe blow to her, and she was not yet able, even had she been willing, to say anything.

"That's very nice of you, Dolly," called Mary Turner. "But it isn't so at all. You sailed your boat very cleverly. We didn't think of going off after the wind until it was too late. I think it was mighty plucky of you to keep on when we had such a big lead. Congratulations!"

"Oh, what's the use of talking like that?" cried Gladys, furiously. "It was a trick—that was all it was! If we had had a real wind all the way, we'd have beaten you by half a mile!''

"I know it, Gladys It was a trick," said Dolly, cheerfully. "That's just what I said. We'll have another race, won't we? And we'll pick out a day when the wind is good and strong, so that it will be just the same for both boats."

"Oh, you'd find some other trick to help you win," said Gladys, sulkily. "Don't act like that —it's easy enough for you to be pleasant. They'll all be laughing at me now for not being able to win when I had such a lead "

"I'm ashamed of you, Gladys," said Mary Turner, blushing scarlet. "Dolly, please don't think that any of the rest of us feel as Gladys does. If I'd known she was such a poor loser, I wouldn't have let her race with you at all. And there won't be another race, Gladys doesn't deserve another chance."

"Gladys is quite right," said Dolly, soberly. "It's very easy to be nice and generous when you've won; it's much harder to be fair when you've lost And it was a trick, after all.''

"No, it wasn't, Dolly," said Eleanor, seriously. "It was perfectly fair. It was good strategy, but it wasn't tricky at all. Gladys knew just as much about the wind as you did If she had done as you did in time, instead of waiting until after she'd seen you do it, she would have won the race ''

"We're going to have trouble with that Gladys Cooper yet," said Margery. "She's spoiled, and she's got a nasty disposition to start with, anyhow. You'd better look out, Dolly. She'll do anything she can to get even.''

"I think this race was one of the things she thought would help her to get even," said Bessie. "She was awfully sure she was going to be able to beat you, Dolly ''

"I almost wish she had," said Dolly. "I don't mean that I would have done anything to let her win, of course, because there wouldn't be any fun about that. But what's an old race, anyhow?''

"That's the right spirit, Dolly," said Eleanor. "It's the game that counts, not the result. We ought to play to win, of course, but we ought to play fair first of all. And I think that means not doing anything at all that would spoil the other side's chances."

"Oh, that's all right," said Margery, "but I'm glad we won."

"I'm glad," said Dolly. "And I'm sorry, too. That sounds silly, doesn't it, but it's what I mean. Maybe if Gladys had won, we could have patched things up. And now there'll be more trouble than ever."

While they talked they were furling the *Eleanor's* sails, and soon they were ready to go ashore. Dolly had brought them up cleverly beside the skiff, and, once the anchor was dropped and everything on board the swift little sloop had been made snug for the night, they dropped over into the skiff and rowed to the beach. There the other girls, who had been greatly excited during the race, and were overjoyed by the result, greeted them with the Wo-he-lo song. Zara, especially, seemed delighted.

"I felt so bad that I cried when I thought you were going to be beaten," she said. "Oh, Bessie, I'm glad you won! And I bet it was because you were on board."

Bessie laughed.

"You'd better not let Dolly hear you say that," she said. "I didn't have a thing to do with it, Zara. It was all Dolly's cleverness that won that race."

"I'm awfully glad you're back, Bessie. I've had the strangest feeling this afternoon—as if someone were watching me."

Bessie grew grave at once. Although she never shared them, she had grown chary of laughing at Zara's premonitions and feelings. They had been justified too often by what happened after she spoke of them.

"What do you mean, dear?" she asked. "I don't see how anyone could be around without being seen. It's very open."

"I don't know, but I've had the feeling, I'm sure of that. It's just as if someone had known exactly what I was doing, as long as I was out here on the beach. But when I went into the tent, it stopped. That made me feel that I must be right "

"Well, maybe you're mistaken, Zara. You know we've had so many strange things happen to us lately that it would be funny if it hadn't made you nervous. You're probably imagining this."

Though Bessie tried thus to disarm Zara's suspicions, she was by no means easy in her own mind. She felt that it would be a good thing to induce Zara to forget her presentiment, or feeling, or whatever it was, if she could. But, just the same, she determined to be on her guard, and she spoke to Dolly.

"She's a queer case, that Zara," said Dolly, with a little shiver. "If any other girl I knew said anything like that, I'd just laugh at her. But Zara's different, somehow. She seems sort of mysterious. Perhaps it's just because she's a foreigner—I don't know."

"I spoke to you so that we could be on the lookout, Dolly. And I guess we'd better not say anything to anyone else. I think a lot of the girls would laugh at Zara if they knew that she had such ideas."

Bessie and Dolly managed to find occasion to cover most of the beach before supper, and they went up to the spring at the top of the bluff that overlooked the beach. The water had been piped down, and there was no longer any need of carrying pails up there to get water, but it was still a pleasant little walk, for the view from the top of the path was delightful. And Bessie and Dolly remembered, moreover, that it was there that the men who had watched the camp on the night of the fire had hidden themselves. But this time they found no one there.

Supper was a merry meal. The race of the afternoon was, of course, the principal topic of conversation, and in addition there were adventures to be told by those who had missed it and gone into Bay City to shop.

But Bessie, watching Zara, noticed toward the end of the meal that her strange little friend, who happened to be sitting near the entrance of the tent in which they ate, was nervous and kept looking behind her out into the darkness as if she saw something. And so, with a whispered explanation to Dolly, she rose and crept very silently toward the door. As she passed Zara, she let her hand fall reassuringly on her shoulder, and then, gathering herself, sprang out into the night.

And, so completely surprised by her sudden appearance that he could not get out of the way, there was Jake Hoover! Jake Hoover, who was supposed to be in the city, telling his story to Charlie Jamieson! Jake Hoover, who, after having done all sorts of dirty work for Holmes and his fellow-conspirators, had told Bessie that he was sorry and was going to change sides!

"Jake!" said Bessie, sternly. "You miserable sneak! What are you doing here?"

No wonder poor Zara had had that feeling of
being watched.   Jake's work for Holmes right
along had been mostly that of the spy, and
here he was once more engaged in it.   Bessie
was furious at her discovery.   Big and
strong as Jake was, he was whimpering now,
and Bessie seized him and shook him by the
shoulders.

"Tell me what you're doing here right away!"
commanded Bessie.   Gone were the days when she
had feared him—the well-remembered days of her
bondage on the Hoover farm, when his word had
always been enough to secure her punishment at
the hands of his mother, who had never been able
to see the evil nature of her boy.

"I ain't doin' no harm—honest I ain't, Bessie,"
he whined.   "I—jest wanted—I jest wanted to see
you and Miss Mercer—honest, that's why I'm
here!"

"That's a likely story, isn't it?" said Bessie,
scornfully.   "If that was so, why did you come
sneaking around like this?   Why didn't you come

right out and ask for us? You didn't think **we** were going to eat you, did you?"

"I—I didn't want them to know I was doin' it, Bess," he said "I'm scared, Bessie—I'm afraid of what they'd do to me, if they found out I **was** takin' your side agin' them."

Despite herself, Bessie felt a certain pity **for** the coward coming over her. She released **his** shoulder, and stood looking at him with infinite scorn in her eyes

"And to think I was ever afraid of you!" **she** said, aloud.

"That's right, Bess," he said, pleadingly. "**I** wouldn't hurt you—you know that, don't you? I used to like to tease you and worry you a bit, but I never meant any real harm. I was always good to you, mostly, wasn't I?"

"Dolly!" called Bessie, sharply She didn't know just what to do, and she felt that, having Jake here, he should be held. It had been **plain** that Charlie Jamieson had considered what he **had** **to** tell valuable.

"Hello! Did you call me, Bessie?" said Dolly, coming out of the tent. "Oh!"

The exclamation was wrung out of her as she saw and recognized Jake.

"So he's spying around here now, is he?" she said. "I told you he was a bad lot when you let him go at Windsor, didn't I? I knew he'd be up to his old tricks again just as soon as he got half a chance"

"Never mind that, Dolly. Tell Miss Eleanor he's here, will you, and ask her to come out? I think she'd better see him, now that he's here."

" That's right—and, say, tell her to hurry, will you?" begged Jake. "I can't stay here—I'm afraid they'll catch me."

Dolly went into the tent again, and in a moment Eleanor Mercer came out. She had never seen Jake before, but she knew all about him for Bessie and Zara had told her enough of his history for her to be more intimate with his life than his own parents

"Good evening, Jake," she said, as she saw

him. "So you decided to talk to us instead of to Mr. Jamieson? Well, I'm glad you're here. I'll have to keep you waiting a minute, but I shan't be long. Stay right there till I come back."

"Yes, ma'am," whined Jake. "But do hurry, please, ma'am! I'm afraid of what they'll do to me if they find I'm here."

Eleanor was gone only a few minutes, and when she returned she was smiling, as if at some joke that she shared with no one.

" I'm sure you haven't had any supper, Jake," she said. "The girls have finished. See, they're coming out now. Come inside, and I'll see that you get a good meal. You'll be able to talk better when you've eaten."

Jake hesitated, plainly struggling between his hunger and his fear. But hunger won, and he went into the tent, followed by Bessie and Dolly, who, although the service was reluctant on Dolly's part, at least, saw to it that he had plenty to eat.

"Just forget your troubles and pitch into that

food, Jake," said Eleanor, kindly. "You'll be able to talk much better on a full stomach, you know "

And whenever Jake seemed inclined to stop eating, and to break out with new evidences of his alarm, they forced more food on him. At last, however, he was so full that he could eat no more, and he rose nervously.

"I've got to be going now," he said. "Honest, I'm afraid to stay here any longer—"

"Oh, but you came here to tell us something, you know," said Eleanor. "Surely you're not going away without doing that, are you?"

"I did think you'd keep your word, Jake," said Bessie, reproachfully

"I can't! I've got to go, I tell you!" Jake broke out. His fright was not assumed; it was plain that he was terrified. "If they was after you, I guess you'd know—here, I'm going—"

"Not so fast, young man!" said a stern voice in the door of the tent, and Jake almost collapsed as Bill Trenwith, a policeman in uniform at his back, came in. "There you are, Jones, there's your man   Arrest him on a charge of having no means of support—that will hold him for the present   We can decide later on what we want to send him to prison for. He's done enough to get him twenty years.''

Jake gave a shriek of terror and fell to the ground, grovelling at the lawyer's feet.

"Oh, don't arrest me!" he begged. "I'll tell you everything I know. Don't arrest me!"

"It's the only way to hold you," said Trenwith   "You've got to learn to be more afraid of us than of Holmes.''

CHAPTER X

"You're a fine lot," declared Jake, something about Trenwith's manner seeming to steady him so that he could talk intelligibly. "You tell me I won't get into any trouble if I come here, and then I find it's a trap!"

"No one told you anything of the sort, my lad," said Trenwith, sharply. "You promised to go to Mr. Jamieson and tell him what you knew No one made you any promises at all, except that you were told you wouldn't have any reason to regret doing it"

Jake looked at Eleanor balefully.

"She's too sharp, that's what she is," he complained bitterly. "I might ha' known she was playing a trick on me—gettin' me to stay here and eat a fine supper. I suppose she went and sent word to you while I was doing it"

"Of course I did, Jake," said Eleanor quietly. "I telephoned to Mr. Trenwith even before you had your supper because I knew that if I didn't do something to keep you here with us, you'd run away again But I did it as much for your sake as for Bessie's "

"Yes, you did—not!" said Jake. "Why shouldn't you let me go now, then, if that is so?"

"Listen to me, my buck," said Trenwith, sternly. "You're not going to do yourself any good by getting fresh to this lady, I can tell you that. You're pretty well scared, aren't you? You told her that you were afraid of what Holmes would do to you?"

But Jake, alarmed by Trenwith's mention of the name of the man he reared, shut his lips obstinately, and wouldn't say a word in answer. Trenwith smiled cheerfully.

"Oh, you needn't talk now, unless you want to," he said. "I know all you could tell me about that, anyhow. You've been up to some mischief, and they've kept on telling you that if you didn't behave yourself they'd give you away."

Jake's hangdog look showed that to be true, although he still maintained his obstinate silence.

"Well, I happen to be charged with enforcing the law around here, and it's my duty to see that criminals are brought to justice. I don't know just what you've done, but I'll find out, and I'll see that you are turned over to the proper authorities—unless you can do something that will make it worth while to let you off. So, you see, you've got just as much reason to be afraid of us as of the gang you've been training with

"They won't be able to help you now, either, even if they should want to—and I don't believe they want to, when it comes to that. I've always found that crooks will desert their best friends if it seems to them that they'll get something out of doing it So if you're trusting to them to get you out of this scrape, you're making a big mistake."

"You'd better listen to what Mr. Trenwith says, Jake," said Eleanor. "You think I've led you into a trap here. Well, I have, in a way. You'll have to go to jail for a little while, anyhow. But you're safer there than you would be if you were free. We're all willing to be your friends, for your father's sake. If we can, we'll get you out of this trouble you are in   But you will have to help us. Think it over.''

"What's the use?" said Jake, sullenly. "I ain't got nothin' to tell you, because I don't know nothin'. An' if I did—"

"You'd better take him along, Jones," said Trenwith to the policeman. "It's quite evident that we'll get nothing out of him to-night. And I don't see any use wasting time on him while he's in this frame of mind."

And so Jake, whining and protesting, was taken away. As soon as he was out of sight and hearing Trenwith's manner changed

"By George," he said, excitedly, "that's a good piece of work! There's something mighty interesting coming off here pretty soon. I'm not at liberty to tell you what it is yet, but 1 had a long talk on the telephone with Charlie just before you called me, Eleanor, and there are going to be ructions!"

"Oh, I suppose we mustn't ask you to tell us, if you've promised not to do it," said Eleanor, "but I do wish we knew!"

She didn't seem to notice that he had called her by her first name—a privilege that was not accorded, as a rule, to those who had no more of an acquaintance with her than Billy Trenwith. But he had done it so naturally, and with so little thought, that she could hardly have resented it, anyway. But Dolly noticed it, and nudged Bessie mischievously.

"Then you really think we're going to find something out from Jake, Mr. Trenwith?" asked Dolly.

"We'll find a way to make him talk, never fear," said Trenwith. "The boy's a natural born coward. He'll do anything to save his own skin if he finds he's in real trouble and that the others of his gang can't help him. I don't think he's naturally bad or vicious—I think he's just weak. He was spoiled by his mother, wasn't he? He acts the way a good many boys do who have been treated that way. He's not got enough strength of character to keep him from taking the easiest path. If a thing seems safe, he's willing to do it to avoid trouble.''

"You know there's just one thing that occurs to me,'' said Eleanor, looking worried. "Jake may have come here with some vague idea of telling us what he knew. But suppose he has seen Holmes or some of the others since Bessie got him to promise to go to Charlie Jamieson in the city?''

"I hoped you wouldn't think of that,'' said Trenwith, gravely. "I thought of it, too. You mean he might have been here just as a spy, with no idea of showing himself at all?''

"The way he acted makes it look as if that was just why he was here, too,'' said Dolly. "He was sneaking around, and he certainly didn't seem very pleased when Bessie found him.''

"He did his best to squirm away," said Bessie. "If Zara hadn't been so nervous while we were eating supper I would never have thought of going after him, either. But she seems to be able to see things and hear things, in some queer fashion, when no one else can "

"That's a good thing for the rest of us," said Trenwith with a smile. "She's a useful person to have around at a time like this I'm going to have a couple of my men—detectives—stay around here to-night to keep an eye on things. It's likely, of course, that there's nothing to be afraid of, but just the same, we don't want to take any chances."

"I'm glad you've done that," said Eleanor. "I don't think I'm the ordinary type of timid woman, but I must confess that all these things worry me, and I'll feel a lot safer if I know that we are not entirely at the mercy of any trick they try to play on us to-night. They seem to be getting bolder all the time."

"Well, after all you know, that's one of the most hopeful things about the whole business.

It means that they're getting desperate—that their time is getting short They feel that if they don't succeed soon they never will, because it will be too late. All we've got to do is to stand them off a little longer, and the whole business will be settled and done with.

"I've got to get back to Bay City to-night. If anything happens, don't hesitate to call me up, no matter what time it is. If I'm out at any time you do have to call me, I'll leave word where I'm going, so that if you tell them at my house who you are, they'll find me. Good-night!"

Neither Dolly nor Bessie slept well that night. Jake's appearance had been disturbing; it seemed to both of them much more likely that his coming heralded some new attempt by Holmes, rather than a desire on his part to confess But the night passed without anything to rouse them, and in the morning their fears seemed rather foolish, as fears are apt to do when they are examined in the sunlight of a new day.

"I don't see what they can do, after all," said

Dolly. "There aren't any woods around here as there were at Long Lake. We're all in sight of the camp and of one another all the time, and they certainly won't be able to work that trick of setting the tents on fire again "

"I guess you're right," said Bessie. "It seems different this morning, somehow. I was worried enough last night but I feel a whole lot better now. I'm glad it's such a beautiful day. The weather makes a lot of difference in the way you feel. It always does with me, I know."

"I'm going out in the sloop after breakfast," said Dolly. "That is, if Miss Eleanor says it's all right There's a lot more wind than there was yesterday, and we can have some good fun."

"Can I go, too?" asked Bessie. "You were quite right when you told me I'd love the sea-shore, Dolly Do you remember how I said I was sorry we were leaving the mountains?"

"Oh, I knew it would fascinate you, just as it does me. So you've given up your love for the mountains?"

"Not a bit of it! I love them as much as ever, but I've found out that the seashore has attractive things about it, too. And I think sailing, the way we did yesterday, is about the nicest of all "

"Then you just wait until we get out there to-day, with a real breeze, and a good sea running That's going to be something you've never even dreamed of "

They had hearty appetites for breakfast in spite of their restless and disturbed sleep, for the bracing effects of their swim, taken before the meal, more than made up for the lack of proper rest And after breakfast Dolly asked permission to go out in the sloop, since one of the very few rules of the Camp Fire, and one strictly enforced, had to do with water sports.

None of the girls were ever allowed to go in swimming unless the Guardian was present, and the same rules applied to boating and sailing— with the added restriction that no girl who did not know how to swim well enough to pass certain tests was allowed to go in a boat at all. Moreover, bathing suits had always to be worn when in a boat.

"Indeed you may," said Eleanor, when Dolly asked her question "And will you take me with you? I'd like to be out on that sea to-day. It looks glorious."

"We'll love to have you along," said Dolly. "How soon may we start?"

"It's eight o'clock," said Eleanor, looking at her watch "We can start at ten. That will allow plenty of time after eating Of course, we don't intend to go in the water, but you never can tell—it's squally today, and we might be upset And that's one thing I don't believe in taking chances with. A cramp will make the best swimmer in the world perfectly helpless in the water, and about every case of cramps I ever heard of came from going in the water too soon after a meal."

When they were aboard the *Eleanor* and scooting through the opening in the bar, Bessie found that the conditions were indeed very different from

those of the previous afternoon The wind had
changed and become much heavier, and as the
Eleanor went along, she dipped her bow con-
tinually, so that the spray rose and drenched all
on board. But there was something splendidly
exciting and invigorating about it, and she loved
every new sensation that came to her.

"Here's the *Defiance* coming out," said Eleanor,
after they had been enjoying the sport for half
an hour. "Gladys must like this sort of a breeze,
too."

"She does, but she's never had as much of it as
I have," said Dolly. "I hope she understands it
well enough not to make any mistakes A boat
like this takes a good deal of handling in a heavy
breeze, and it seems to me that she's carrying a
good deal of sail."

"She seems to be getting along all right,
though," said Eleanor, after watching the *Defiance*
for a few minutes. "Why, Dolly, I wonder what
she's doing now."

The maneuvres of the *Defiance* seemed strange

enough to prompt Eleanor's question, for, no matter how Dolly tacked, the *Defiance* followed her, drawing nearer all the time. Since Dolly had no sort of definite purpose in mind, it was plain that Gladys was simply following her And soon the reason was apparent

"She's trying to race, she wants to show that she can beat us to-day when there's plenty of wind," said Dolly "If she wanted to race, why didn't she say so?"

"Well, give her her way, Dolly," said Eleanor. "Keep straight on now for a little while and see if she can beat you We're just about on even terms now."

And on even terms they stayed. Sometimes one, sometimes the other seemed to gain a little ad- vantage, but it was plain that the boats, as well as the skippers, were very evenly matched Since there was no agreement to race, Dolly had the choice of courses, and in a spirit of mischief she came about frequently. And every time she changed her course Gladys followed suit.

Although the boats were often within easy hailing distance, Gladys avoided Dolly's eyes, and nothing was said by those on either sloop They were satisfied with the fun of this impromptu racing But at last, when they were perhaps a mile from the opening in the bar, and very close together, Eleanor, looking at her watch, saw that it was nearly time for lunch.

"You'd better turn for home now, Dolly," she said. " Suppose I give Gladys a hail and suggest a race to the bar?"

"All right," agreed Dolly.

"Gladys!" Eleanor sent her clear voice across the water, and Gladys answered with a wave of her hands She seemed in better humor than she had been the day before.

"We're going in now. Want to race to the bar?"

"All right!" called Gladys, in answer and came about smartly. She had been quick, but Dolly was just as quick, and they were on the most even terms imaginable as the race began.

But Dolly and the *Eleanor* had one advantage
that Gladys was not slow to recognize. The
Eleanor had the inside course In a close finish
that would be very likely to spell the difference between victory and defeat, since, to reach the opening, Gladys would either have to get far enough
ahead to cross the *Eleanor's* bows or else to cross
behind her, which would entail so much loss of
time that Dolly would be certain to bring her
craft home a winner. But since the previous racing had shown the *Defiance* to be just a trifle
swifter before the wind, that advantage seemed
to be one that Gladys could easily overcome

Now that she was racing, however, Dolly
changed her tactics. Fresh as the wind was, she
shook out a reef in her mainsail, and as they neared
the bar the *Eleanor* actually carried more canvas
than Gladys dared to keep on the *Defiance*. Being
less used to heavy going than Dolly, she was not so
sure of the strength of her sticks, and reckless
though she was, she was too wise to be willing to
take a chance of being dismasted.

And so the advantage that Gladys had to gain to be able to cross the *Eleanor's* bows seemed to be impossible for her to attain The *Eleanor* did not go ahead, but she held her own, and she had the right of way.

"You're going to beat her again, and fair and square this time," said Eleanor, excitedly. "She won't be able to say a word to this!"

"Look!" said Dolly, suddenly. "She's going to cross me—and she's got no right to do it!" She shouted loudly. "Gladys! Gladys! I'll run you down! Don't do that! I've got the right of way!"

But Gladys kept on with a mocking laugh. Furious at the trick, Dolly put her helm hard over, and the *Eleanor* came up in the wind.

"That's a mean trick, if you like!" cried Dolly, indignantly. "In a regular race, if she did a thing like that, the other boat would run her down, and would win on a foul. But she knew very well I'd give up the position rather than cause an accident!"

The check to the *Eleanor* was only for a moment, but it was enough to throw her off her course and make it certain that the *Defiance* would reach the bar first.

"Never mind, Dolly. You did the right thing," said Eleanor, quietly. "I think she's quite welcome to the race, if she cares enough about winning it to play a trick like that!"

Bessie was up in the bow, looking intently at the *Defiance*. And now as Gladys came up to get the straight course again, something went wrong. By some mistaken handling of her helm she had lost her proper direction, and to her amazement Bessie saw the boom come over sharply. She saw it, too, strike Gladys on the head—and the next moment the *Defiance* gybed helplessly, while Gladys was swept overboard.

Bessie did not hesitate a moment. She had seen that blow struck by the boom, and with a cry of warning she plunged overboard as they swept by the helpless *Defiance*, and with powerful strokes made for the place where Gladys had gone overboard. Gladys had gone straight down, but Bessie had marked the spot, and she dived as she reached it, and met her coming up. She clutched her in a moment, and was on the surface almost at once, holding Gladys, and looking for Dolly and the *Eleanor*. Dolly would return for her at once, she knew, if she had seen Gladys go over. But, to her amazement the sloop was heading for the bar, sailing away from her fast! Dolly had not seen her and, for a moment, Bessie was badly scared.

CHAPTER XI

In a moment, however, she realized that she could not be left alone for long. Her absence from the *Eleanor* would be noticed, even if no one had seen her leap overboard; and, moreover, the strange behavior of the *Defiance* was sure to attract Dolly's attention, for, without Gladys to direct her, the *Defiance* was in a bad way. She had heeled over sharply, and seemed now to be sailing in circles, following the errant impulses of the wind, which caught first one sail, then another.

Although she was quite near the *Defiance*, Bessie looked for no help from her. To swim toward her, with Gladys as a burden, seemed hopeless. The boat was not staying in one position. And moreover, Marcia Bates and the other girl on board of her seemed almost entirely ignorant of what to do. They would have quite enough on their hands in trying to get her headed for the opening in the bar.

And suddenly a new danger was added to the others. For Gladys, it seemed, was recovering her senses—or, rather, she was no longer unconscious. To her horror, Bessie found, as Gladys opened her eyes, that she was delirious. That, of course, was the effect of the blow on her head from the boom, but its effect, no matter what the cause, was what worried Bessie.

"Keep still! Don't move, Gladys!" warned Bessie, as she saw the other girl's eyes open.

But Gladys either would not or could not obey that good advice. She struggled furiously by way of answer, and for a long minute Bessie was too busy keeping afloat to be able to look for the coming of the help that was so badly needed.

There seemed to be no purpose to the struggles of Gladys, but they were none the less desperate because of that. Her eyes had the wide, fixed stare that, had Bessie known it, is so invariably seen in those who are in mortal fear of drowning. And she clung to Bessie with a strength that no one could have imagined her capable of displaying.

And at last, though she hated to do it, Bessie managed to get her hands free, and, clenching her fists, she drove them repeatedly into the other's face so that Gladys was forced to let go and put her hands before her face to cover herself from the vicious blows.

At once Bessie seized the opportunity. She flung herself away, knowing that even though she did not try to help herself, but being conscious, Gladys would not sink at once, and got behind her, so that she could grasp her by the shoulders and be safe from the deadly clutch of her arms.

Free from the terrible danger that is the risk assumed by all who rescue drowning persons, that of being dragged down by the victim, Bessie was able to raise her head and look for the *Eleanor*. And now she gave a wild cry as she saw the sloop

bearing down upon her. Eleanor Mercer was
in the bow, a coil of rope in her hands, and a
moment later she flung it skillfully, so that
Bessie caught it. At once Bessie made a
noose and slipped the rope over Gladys's shoulders. Then she let go, and, turning on her back,
rested while Gladys was dragged toward the
sloop.

Bessie herself was almost exhausted by her
struggle. She felt that, had her very life depended upon doing it, she could not have swam
the few yards that separated her from the sloop.
But there was no need for her to do it. Steering with the utmost skill, Dolly soon brought the
Eleanor alongside of Bessie as she lay floating
in the water, and a moment later she was being
helped aboard.

"Lie down and rest," commanded Eleanor.
"Don't try to talk yet."

And Bessie was glad enough to obey. She lay
down beside Gladys, who seemed to have fainted
again, and Eleanor threw a rug over her.

"Now we must get them ashore as quickly as we can, Dolly," said Eleanor. "Bessie's just tired out, but I don't like the looks of Gladys at all."

"The boom hit her," said Bessie, weakly. "It hit her on the head. That's how she was knocked overboard. She didn't know what she was doing when she struggled so in the water."

"What a lucky thing you saw what happened!" said Dolly. "I was so intent on the race that I never looked at all, and I didn't even know you'd gone over until I called to you and you didn't answer."

"Oh, I knew you'd come back, Dolly. I just wondered, when Gladys was struggling so, if you'd be in time."

This time Dolly didn't stop at the anchorage of the sloop, but ran her right up on the beach. That meant some trouble in getting her off when they came to that, but it was no time to hesitate because of trifles. Once they were ashore, the other girls, who had, of course, seen nothing of the accident

that had so nearly had a tragic ending, rushed up
to help, and in a few moments Gladys was being
carried to the big living tent.

There her wet clothes were taken off, she was
rubbed with alcohol, and wrapped in hot blankets.
And as Eleanor and Margery Burton stood over
her, she opened her eyes, looked at them in
astonishment, and wanted to know where she
was.

"Oh, thank Heaven!" cried Eleanor. "She's
come to her senses, I do believe! Gladys, do you
feel all right?"

"I—I— think so," said Gladys, faintly, putting
her hand to her head. "I've got an awful headache. What happened? I seem to remember being hit on the head—"

"Your boom struck you as it swung over, and
knocked you into the water, Gladys," said Eleanor. "You couldn't swim, and you don't remember anything after that, do you? It dazed you
for a time, so that you didn't know what you
were doing. But you're all right now, though

I've telephoned for a doctor, and he'd better
have a look at you when he comes, just to make
sure you're all right.''

"But—how did I get here?''

"Bessie King saw you go overboard and jumped
after you. Of course, the girls on your boat were
pretty helpless—she was going all around in circles after you left the tiller free, so they couldn't
do anything ''

Gladys closed her eyes for a moment.

"I'd like to talk to her later—when I feel better,'' she said. "I think I'll try to go to sleep
now, if I may. The pain in my head is dreadful ''

"Yes, that's the best thing you can do,'' said
Eleanor warmly. "You'll feel ever so much better, I know, when you wake up. Someone will be
here with you all the time, so that if you wake
up and want anything, you'll only need to ask
for it.''

But Gladys was asleep before Eleanor had finished speaking. Nature was taking charge of the

case and prescribing the greatest of all her remedies, sleep.

Eleanor turned away, with relief showing plainly in her eyes.

"I think she'll be all right now," she said "If that blow were going to have any serious effects, I don't believe she'd be in her senses now."

"I think it's a good thing it happened, in a way," said Dolly, when they were outside of the tent. "Did you notice how she spoke about Bessie, Miss Eleanor?"

"Yes. I see what you mean, Dolly. Of course, I'm sorry she had to have such an experience, but maybe you're right, after all. I'm quite sure that her feelings toward Bessie will be changed after this—she'd have to be a dreadful sort of girl if she could keep on cherishing her dislike and resentment. And I'm sure she's not "

"Hello! Why aren't you in bed, sleeping off that ducking?" asked Dolly suddenly. For Bessie, in dry clothes, and looking as if she had had nothing more exciting than an ordinary plunge into the sea to fill her day, was coming toward them from her own tent.

"Oh, I feel fine!" said Bessie. "The only trouble with me was that I was scared—just plain scared! If I'd known that everything was going to be all right, I could have turned and swam ashore after you started towing Gladys in. Is she all right? I'm more bothered about her than about myself."

"I think she's going to feel a lot better when she wakes up," said Eleanor. "I think I'm enough of a doctor to be able to tell when there's anything seriously wrong. But I'm not taking any chances—I've sent for a doctor."

"How about the other boat? Did they get in all right?" asked Dolly. "I forgot all about them, I was so worked up about Bessie and Gladys."

"They had a tough time, but they managed it," said Margery Burton. "Here's Miss Turner now. I suppose she's worried about Gladys."

Worried she certainly was, but Eleanor was

able to reassure her, and soon the doctor, arriving from Green Cove, pronounced Gladys to be in no danger.

"She'll have that headache when she wakes up," he said; "but it will be a lot better, and by to-morrow morning it will be gone altogether. Don't give her much to eat, some chicken broth ought to be enough. She's evidently got a good constitution. If she had fractured her skull she wouldn't have been conscious yet, nor for a good many days."

But the accident had one unforeseen consequence, that was rather amusing than otherwise to Dolly, at first, at least. For, before the doctor was ready to go, the sound of an automobile engine was heard up on the bluff, and a minute later Billy Trenwith came racing down the path

At the sight of Eleanor he paused, looking a little sheepish.

"I heard that Doctor Black was coming here —I was afraid something might have happened to you," he stammered.

"Why, whatever made you think that?" said Eleanor, honestly puzzled. Then she turned, surprised again by a burst of hysterical laughter from Dolly, who, staring at Trenwith's red face, was entirely unable to contain her mirth. Under Eleanor's steady gaze she managed to control herself, but then she went off again helplessly as Doctor Black winked at her very deliberately.

Scandalized and rather indignant as the point of the joke began to reach her, Eleanor was dismayed to see that Bessie, the grave, was also having a hard time to keep from laughing outright. So she blushed, which was the last thing in the world she wanted to do, and then made some excuse for a hasty flight.

"Well, you people have so many things happen to you all the time," said Trenwith, indignantly, " that I don't see why it wasn't perfectly natural for me to come out to see what was wrong now!"

"Oh, don't apologize to me, Mr. Trenwith!"

said Dolly, mischievously. "And—can you keep a secret?"

He looked at her, not knowing whether he ought to laugh or frown, and Dolly went up to him, put her hands on his shoulders, and raised herself so that she could whisper in his ear.

"She isn't half as angry as she pretends," she said.

Then Eleanor came back, and Dolly made herself scarce. She had a positive genius for knowing just how far she could go safely in her teasing.

"I had to come out here, anyhow," said Trenwith, to Eleanor. "Look here. I got this message from Charlie Jamieson."

Eleanor took it.

"I don't see why you let Charlie order you around so," she said, severely. "Haven't you any business of your own to attend to? He hasn't any right to expect you to waste all your time trying to keep us out of trouble."

"Oh, it isn't wasted," he said, indignantly.

"We're supposed to help our friends—and we're friends, aren't we?"

"Of course we are," said Eleanor, relenting

He brightened at once.

"Well," he said, impulsively, "you see Charlie says he doesn't want me to let you and those two girls—Bessie and Zara—out of my sight until he comes. Couldn't you all come out for a sail with me in my motor launch? We could have supper on board and it would be lots of fun, I think."

Eleanor looked doubtful

"I don't know about leaving the camp," she said "I ought to be here to keep an eye on things."

"Oh, you can go perfectly well, Miss Eleanor," said Margery Burton. "It will do Bessie and Dolly a lot of good if you take them—they've had a pretty exciting day. And we can ask all the Halsted girls over to supper, and Miss Turner will be with them She can take your place as Guardian for a few hours, can't she?"

"If she will come. Why, yes, that would make

it all right," said Eleanor Somehow she found
that she wasn't half as strong-minded and self-
reliant when this very masterful young man was
around. "You might go over and see, Margery,
if you will "

"Splendid!" said Trenwith. "We'll have a
perfectly bully time, I know. You keep at it too
hard, Miss Mercer—really you do!"

"We won't go very far, will we?" said Eleanor, yielding to the lure of a sail at sunset.

"Oh, no, just a few miles down the coast.
There's a lot of pretty scenery you ought to see—
and I've got a man who helps me to run my boat
who's a perfect wizard at cooking. We've got a
sort of imitation kitchen on board, but he does
things in it that would make the chef of a big
hotel envious. He's one of the few things I boast
about "

Margery soon returned with word that the
Halsted girls would accept the supper invitation,
nd that Mary Turner would be delighted to come.
Margery's eyes were twinkling, and it was plain

that Mary Turner had said something else that was not to be repeated

"All right! That's great!" said Trenwith, happily. "I'll run back to Green Cove in my car, and come around here again in the launch. It was to follow me there I'll be back soon "

Indeed, in half an hour he was back, and Eleanor with Zara, Bessie and Dolly, were taken out to the *Columbia* in two trips of the little dinghy which served as her tender. The *Columbia* was a big, roomy, motor launch, without a deck, but containing a little cabin, and a comfortable lounging space aft, which was covered with an awning.

"What a delightful boat!" said Eleanor, as she settled herself comfortably amid the cushions Trenwith had provided for her. "I should think you could have an awfully good time on her."

"I've used her a lot," said Trenwith. "There's room in the cabin for two fellows to sleep, if they don't mind being crowded, and of course in warm weather one can sleep out here I've used her quite a lot to go duck hunting, and for little cruises

when I've been all tired out. Charlie Jamieson
has been with me several times.''

"I've heard him talk about the good times he's
had on her. It was stupid of me to have forgotten ''

"She's not very fast or very fashionable, but
she is good fun. I'd rather have a steady, slow
engine that you can depend on than one of those
racing motors that's always getting out of order.''

"All ready to start, sir, Mr Trenwith,'' said
Bates, his 'crew,' then, and Trenwith took the
wheel.

"All right,'' he said. "Let her go, Bates! You
can steer from the wheel in the bow after we get
started, right down the coast. We'll lie to off
Humber Island and eat supper.''

· Right, sir!'' said Bates. "I've got a good
suppe for to-night, too.''

"Being right out on the water this way makes
me hungry,'' said Eleanor. "That's good news,
Bates.''

CHAPTER XII

The *Columbia* slowly and steadily made her way down the coast, keeping within a mile or so of the shore. Speed was certainly not her long suit, but she rode the choppy sea more easily than most boats so small would have done, and, since she was not intended for speed, the usual traffic din of the motor was absent. Altogether, she seemed an ideal pleasure boat.

As they went along, Trenwith pointed out the various places of interest along the shore.

"Down this way we get to a part where a lot of rich men have built summer homes," he said. "You see there's a good beach, and they can buy enough land to have it to themselves. It's pretty lonely, in a way, because they're a good long way from the railroad, but they don't seem to mind that."

189

"I suppose not. They've got money enough to keep all the automobiles and yachts they want, so they wouldn't use the railroad anyhow   I never would if I could get around any other way."

As they went on, the coast changed considerably from the familiar character it had at Plum Beach. Cliffs took the place of the bluff, and while the beach was still fine and level, there were rocky stretches at more and more frequent intervals.

"What's the nearest town in this direction?" asked Eleanor.

"Rock Haven," said Trenwith. "That's more of a place than Bay City, because it's quite a seaport. Up at Bay City, you see, we don't amount to much except in the summer time. But Rock Haven is a big place, and most of the people who live there are there all the year round instead of only for three months or so in the summer. You haven't any idea of what a dull old place Bay City is in winter."

"If it's so dull, I shouldn't think you'd stay there."

"Oh, it was a good place for me to get a start, you know. I've been able to get along in politics, and I've done better there than I would have in the city, I suppose. And it's all right for a bachelor, anyhow. He can always get away. If I were married—well, it would be very different then."

"I should think you'd like it much better in the city, though, even if you are a bachelor. Why don't you come there this winter?"

" Perhaps—I'd like—do you want me to come ?"

He leaned forward, as if her answer were the most important thing in the world, and, seeing Dolly's mischievous glance at Bessie, Eleanor blushed slightly.

"I think it would be better for you to be in the city," she said, with dignity.

"Well, I'll tell you a secret then—I'm really bursting with a whole lot of others that I mustn't tell   Charlie's been at me for months to come and be his partner, and I've promised to think it over."

"I think that would be splendid."

"Well, I'm glad to hear you say so, because it

really depends on you whether I shall come or not.''

"Hush!" she said, blushing again, and speaking in so low a tone that only he could hear her. "You mustn't talk like that here—and now. It—it isn't right."

She looked helplessly at Dolly, and Trenwith, understanding, looked as if she had said something that delighted him. Perhaps she had—perhaps she had even meant to do so.

"I'll attend to getting supper ready now, sir, Mr. Trenwith, if you'll take the wheel," said Bates, just then

"All right," said Trenwith, nodding. "Now make a good job of it, Bates. I've been praising you up to the skies."

Bates grinned widely, and disappeared.

No apologies were needed when they came to eat the supper which had been so well heralded. A table was set up in the after part of the boat, and the awning was drawn back so that the stars shone down on them. The *Columbia's* engine was

stopped, and she lay under the lee of Humber
Island, a long, wooded islet that sheltered them
from the strong breeze, making the sea as smooth
as a mill pond. On shore twinkling lights began
to appear, and, some distance away, a glare of
lights in the sky betrayed the location of Rock
Haven

"Oh, this is lovely!" said Eleanor. "I'm so
glad you brought us here, Mr. Trenwith! But
tell me, doesn't anyone live on this island? It's
so beautiful that I should think someone would
surely have built a summer home there long
ago."

"I believe there are people there," said Trenwith "But they are on the other side."

"I'm sorry we have to go home, but I suppose
we really must be starting," said Eleanor, after
suppei. "It's such a heavenly night that it seems
to me it would be perfect just to stay here "

"Wouldn't it? But you're right—we must be
starting back. We'll go on and come around the
other side of this island. You should see it from

all points of view. Scenically, it's our show place
for this whole stretch of coast.''

And so as soon as Bates had finished clearing
off the table he went back to his engine, and the
Columbia slipped along smoothly in the shadow
of the island. But a few minutes later, as they
were gliding along on the seaward side, where the
water was far rougher, there was a sudden jar,
and the next moment the engine stopped.

''Why, what's the matter?'' asked Eleanor, surprised

''Nothing much, probably,'' said Trenwith.
''Bates will have it fixed in a few minutes. The
best engine in the world is apt to get balky at
times—and I must say that mine has chosen a
very good time to misbehave.''

Eleanor chose to ignore the meaning he so
plainly implied, but she was perfectly content
with the explanation, and sat there dreamily, expecting to hear the reassuring whir of the motor
at any moment. But the minutes dragged themselves out, and the only sound that came from the

engine was the tapping of the tools Bates was using. Trenwith frowned.

"This is very strange," he said. "We've never been delayed as long as this since I've had Bates. He usually keeps the motor in perfect running order. I'll just step forward and see what's wrong"

He returned in a few moments, his face grave.

"Bates has some highly technical explanation of what is wrong," he said, seriously "It seems that he needs some tools he hasn't got, in order to grind the valves I'm afraid we'll have to get ashore somehow—he seems to be sure that he can find what he is looking for there."

Eleanor looked rather dismayed.

"It's going to make us terribly late in getting ashore, isn't it?" she asked. "I'm afraid the others will be worried about us."

"No. Bates says that as soon as he gets the tools he wants he will have things fixed up, and he's quite certain that he can get them on the island. He says anyone who has a motor boat will be able to help him out—and they certainly couldn't live here without one ''

"But how on earth are you going to get ashore if the engine won't work?" asked Dolly. "It seems to me that we're stuck out here."

"Oh, you leave that to us!" said Trenwith, cheerfully. "I'm sorry this has happened, but please believe me when I say that it isn't a bit serious."

They soon saw the *Columbia* was to be rescued from her predicament She was fairly near the shore, and now Bates dropped an anchor, and she remained still, swinging slowly on the chain.

"He'll row ashore, you see, hunt up the people, and tell them what he wants," said Trenwith. "Hurry up, Bates! Remember, we've promised to get these young ladies home in good time."

"Right, sir," said Bates, as he lowered the dinghy and dropped into her. " Won't take me long when I find the people on shore—and about five minutes will fix that engine when I get back here again."

He rowed off into the darkness, making for a point of light that showed on shore, and they settled back to wait as patiently as they could for his return.

"Suppose Charlie turns up at the camp while we're gone, and wants you for something important?" asked Eleanor. "Oh, I'm afraid we did wrong in coming!"

"Not a bit of it! Old Charlie will understand. And I know his plans pretty well, so there isn't any danger of this causing any trouble."

It seemed to take longer for Bates to find help than he had expected. At any rate, the greater part of half an hour slipped away before they heard the sound of oars coming toward them.

"Why, there are two men rowing!" said Dolly, curiously. "And that dinghy only has room for one man with oars"

"Probably they decided to send someone out with him to lend him a hand," said Trenwith. "People around these parts are pretty nice to you if you have a breakdown, and I guess it's

partly because they never know when they're going to have one themselves ''

"Well, that ought to make it easier to make
the repairs that are needed," said Eleanor, some-
what relieved "I really am getting worried about
what they'll think at the beach I'm afraid they'll
be sure that something has happened to us ''

"Good evening, Miss Mercer," said a mocking
voice behind her, and she turned with a start to
see Holmes!

"You're late," said Holmes, reproachfully. "I
expected you an hour earlier. But then better
late than never! Ah, I see both of them are with
you! Silas Weeks will be very glad to see you
two, I have no doubt!"

He spoke then to Bessie and Zara, who, terrified by his sudden appearance, were staring at
him

"Mr Trenwith!" said Eleanor, sharply. "You
know who this man is, do you not? And what
our feelings are concerning him? Are you going
to let him stay here?"

"He has no choice, Miss Mercer. Better not ask him too many questions about how you happened to break down right off my island; he would have a hard time convincing you with any story he told Eh, Trenwith?"

"Shut up!" growled Trenwith. "What does all this nonsense mean? Get off my boat!"

"Oh, are you trying to make them believe you didn't know about this? I beg your pardon, Trenwith, I really do! Of course, Miss Mercer, he knows as well as I do that I am within my rights. You are now in a state where certain court orders applying to Bessie King and her little friend Zara are valid—and, knowing that these two girls, who have run away from the courts of this state, are here, I have taken steps to see that they are taken into court. I am a law abiding citizen—I do not like to see the law insulted."

Eleanor was dazed by the suddenness of the blow. To her it seemed an accident; she could not believe that Trenwith could be guilty

of such treachery as Holmes was charging.
But in a moment her faith in him was
shattered

"I'd like to help out your pose, Trenwith,"
Holmes said to him. "But I need you, so you'll
have to come off your perch. You'll have to come
ashore with the others, in case you should change
your mind. I only want two of these girls, but
the others will have to come, too, of course, because if they got away they might make trouble.
You shall be perfectly comfortable, Miss Mercer,
however."

The look in Trenwith's eyes, and the sheepish,
hangdog expression of his whole face made Eleanor gasp. So he had betrayed them! After all,
despite his fine talk, he had been tempted by the
money that Holmes seemed prepared to spend so
lavishly! And he had led Bessie and Zara right
into a trap—a merciless trap, as she knew, from
which escape would be most difficult, if not utterly
impossible.

And in a moment the lingering remnants of her

faith were shattered. For Holmes called out, in a loud tone, at Bates:

"Bates!" he cried. "Come aboard and start that engine! Then you can take your tub right up to the landing pier in front of the house."

"Yes, yes!" said Bates. He sprang aboard, and a moment later the engine, perfectly restored, was started, although nothing had been done to it since Bates went ashore, and, the anchor lifted, the *Columbia* began her brief voyage to the pier.

There had been no accident at all! The breakdown had been a deception, pure and simple, intended to give Bates a chance to go ashore and warn Holmes that his prey was within his reach.

"Oh, how I despise you!" said Eleanor to Trenwith. "Go away, please, so that I won't have to look at you!"

"Eleanor, listen!" he said, in a low whisper, pleadingly. "I can explain—"

"If you think I'm such a fool as to believe anything you tell me now," she said, furiously, "you are very much mistaken!"

He saw that to argue with her was hopeless, and went forward gloomily. In a few minutes they were ashore. Resistance, as Eleanor saw, was hopeless; the only thing to do was to act sensibly, and hope for a chance to escape.

"I have had three rooms arranged for you," said Holmes, when they reached a great rambling house. "They're on the second floor. I think you girls will be comfortable and you would rather, I am sure, have the girls with you. You are in no danger."

CHAPTER XIII

Half a dozen men had come out to the *Columbia* with Holmes and Bates, and now, while Holmes himself disappeared for a minute, beckoning to Trenwith to go with him, the other men watched Eleanor and the three girls. They drew off to a little distance, but they kept their eyes on them.

"They don't look as if they could run very fast," said Dolly, hopefully. "Don't you think we might be able to make a break and get away?"

"Where to, Dolly? This is an island, remember, and we don't know anything about it at all. We wouldn't know where to run, if we did have luck enough to get a good start—and we wouldn't get very far."

"I suppose that's so," said Dolly, her face falling. "Oh, what a horrid shame! Just when everything seemed so nice and peaceful!"

203

"There's one thing," said Eleanor, her face set and stern "They can't hold me forever—or, at least, I don't suppose they can. And someone is going to be sorry for this or my name's not Eleanor Mercer!"

"I don't understand it yet," said Bessie, who, although the capture meant more to her than it did to any of the others, had not given way to her emotions, and seemed as cool and calm as if she had been safely back on Plum Beach.

"It's only too easy to understand," said Eleanor, bitterly. "Charlie was deceived in his friend, Mr. Trenwith. He's just as easy to bribe as Jake Hoover That's all He cares more for money and success than he does for his reputation as an honorable man. I'm disappointed in him—but I suppose I ought not to be surprised"

"Well, I *am* surprised," said Dolly, defiantly "And I'm sure, somehow, that he's all right I think he was just as badly fooled as the rest of us. Mr. Holmes probably wants us to think as badly of him as possible, so that, if he should try to help us, we wouldn't trust him.''

"I wish I could believe that, Dolly. But the evidence against him is too strong, I'm afraid. Hush, we mustn't talk Here is Mr. Holmes coming back. I don't want him to think that we're afraid—it would please him too much ''

With Mr. Holmes, as he came toward them, was a woman in servant's garb, middle aged, and sour in her appearance.

"This woman will attend to you, Miss Mercer," he said. "She will do whatever you tell her— unless it should happen to conflict with the orders she has from me. But she won't talk to you about me, or about this place because she knows that if she does I will find out about it, and she will have reason to regret it ''

"I'm very much pleased by one thing, Mr. Holmes," said Eleanor "You've shown yourself in your true colors at last. I suppose you understand that when I get back to the city I shall see to it that everyone knows the truth about you. I

don't think you will find yourself welcome in the
homes of any decent people after I tell what I
know.''

"I'm sorry, Miss Mercer," he said. "Of course
you must do what you think best. But it really
won't do any good. I could do things a great
deal worse than this, and still, with the money I
happen to have, people would keep on fawning on
me, and pestering me with their attentions and
their invitations as much as ever."

"Perhaps you're right, but I intend to find out.
May I ask how long you intend to keep me here
as a prisoner?''

"You are my guest, Miss Mercer, not my pris
oner. Please don't act as if I were as great a
villain as that. Losing your temper will not improve matters in any way, you know—really it
won't. As for your question, I think Bessie and
Zara will be in the quite competent care of their
old friend Silas Weeks by noon to-morrow and
then there will be no further reason for keeping
you here ''

"Then, unless you are remarkably quick in getting out of the country, Mr. Holmes, you ought to be under arrest for kidnapping by to-morrow night "

Holmes laughed.

"Oh, do let's be friends!' he said. "You and your friends have really given me a lot of trouble. But do I bear you any malice? Not I! If you hadn't taken care of those misguided girls after they ran away from Hedgeville, none of this would have come about."

"I suppose you think you have some excuse for acting in this fashion?"

"I certainly have, Miss Mercer. The very best. After all, why shouldn't I tell you? It's too late for you to do me any harm now—I have won the game."

"But there will be a return match. Don't forget that! My father is as rich as you are, Mr. Holmes, and when he hears of the way I have been treated, he will spend his last cent, if necessary, to get his revenge on you."

"Dear me, I hope he won't do anything so foolish, Miss Mercer! It would be a dreadful waste of money—and he wouldn't get it, in any case. However, I don't want you to be needlessly worried Zara will soon be safe with her father. She won't have to stay very long with the estimable Farmer Weeks. You know, I really don't blame her for disliking him."

Zara gave a little cry of joy.

"Will I see my father? Is he well?" she cried.

"Quite well—but very obstinate," said Holmes. "That's your fault, too, Miss Mercer. I'm sorry to say that lately he has seemed to be inclined to listen to your cousin, Mr. Jamieson. He is willing, you see, to deal with whoever happens to be in charge of his daughter. He knows our friend Silas very well—too well, I think. And so, when he knows that Zara is being looked after by him, I think he will be glad to meet my terms, and so secure his freedom."

"You brute!" said Eleanor, hotly. "What are your terms?"

"Ah, that would be telling! You will have to wait to discover that. You see, Silas Weeks wasn't quite as stupid as the rest of the people at Hedgeville, and when he couldn't find out what old Slavin was doing there, he came to me—because he thought I probably could "

"Slavin!" said Eleanor, in an amazed tone. "Is that your father's name, Zara? Why didn't you tell us?"

"He told me not to," said Zara, nervously.

"Zara's father had one bad fault; he wasn't at all ready to trust people," Holmes went on, easily. "He didn't even trust me as he should have done, and he's been positively insulting to Weeks. It's made a lot of trouble for him."

He looked at his watch, then turned to the servant.

"Go upstairs and make the rooms comfortable for Miss Mercer at once," he said. "It's getting late." Then he turned to the men who had accompanied him to the *Columbia*. "It's all right, boys," he said "You needn't wait."

"These people keep their ears entirely too wide open," he explained to Eleanor "I have to be rather careful with them, though they probably wouldn't understand much if they did hear Well, that is about all I've got to tell you, anyhow. You see, you needn't worry about your friend Zara. As to Bessie—Well, that's different "

He looked at Bessie malevolently.

"I don't think I care to tell you anything more about her," he said. "Weeks will look after her all right—as well as she deserves to be looked after."

Bessie seemed to be nervous as he looked at her, and edged away from him

"If you think you can keep Bessie in the care of that man Weeks," said Eleanor, "you are going to find yourself decidedly mistaken. He won't treat her properly, and if he doesn't, the courts won't compel her to stay there. I know enough law for that, and I tell you now, that, even though you may have some sort of law on your side just now, because you have played this trick, you won't be able to count on the law much longer. It will be as powerful against you, properly used, as it has been for you, improperly used "

"Oh!" Holmes laughed, unpleasantly. There was no mirth in the laugh, only mockery and contempt. "Really, Miss Mercer—why, where has that little baggage gone to?"

He stared wildly about the room, and Eleanor, startled, looked about her also Bessie had disappeared; vanished into thin air In a rage, Holmes darted here and there about the great hall of the house in which they had been standing. But, though he looked behind curtains and all the larger pieces of furniture, and made a great fuss, he found no sign of her For a moment he was completely baffled, and almost beside himself with rage

"I always thought villains were clever," said Dolly, as he stood still. Her voice was scornful. "Why, even a girl like Bessie can fool you! She's done it plenty of times before now—you didn't think you could keep her from doing it this time, too, did you?"

"What do you mean?" stormed Holmes, moving toward her, his hand raised as if he meant to strike her. But if he thought he could frighten Dolly he was much mistaken. She faced him calmly.

"You can't make me tell you anything, even if you do hit me," she said. "And you won't find Bessie, either, unless she wants you to. I saw her go—but I'm not going to tell you how she managed it."

"Oh, I'm not going to hit her," yelled Holmes. "What good would that do?"

He sprang to a bell, and pushed it violently. In a moment two or three of the men he had dismissed, thus giving Bessie her chance to escape, answered his summons, and he ordered them to start in search of her at once.

"Find her, and you'll be rewarded," he shouted. "But if you don't, I'll make you pay for it!"

Eleanor had never seen a man in such a furious

rage It was plain that his plan, successful as it seemed to be, was still in danger of being upset, and the knowledge gave Eleanor new hope. It had seemed to her that, with Trenwith turned traitor, there was not one chance in a million to foil Holmes this time But now everything was changed. He stayed with them only long enough to give them into the keeping of the servant, who came down the stairs just as he finished giving his orders to the men for the pursuit of Bessie.

"If any of them get out, I'll know it's your fault," he said to her. "And you know what I can do to you. You wouldn't like to go to jail for a few years, I guess. You will, if anyone else gets away from this house to-night."

Then he followed the men he had sent out in search of Bessie.

And all the time Bessie herself had heard every word, and seen every action of the scene that followed the discovery of her escape While Holmes was talking to Eleanor she had seized the chance to slip over to a heavily curtained window, which, she guessed, must open right on the ground.

She took the chance of it being open, and fortune favored her. Concealed by the curtain, she was able to slip out, and then, instead of running as fast and as far as she could, as nine people out of ten would have done, she stayed where she was. She reasoned that there, so close to the house, was the last place where search would be made.

And she was right. She saw Holmes dash from the room; she saw Eleanor and the other girls being led upstairs. And then she not only heard, but saw the pursuit of her that was begun. Men with lanterns searched the grounds; they looked behind every bush. But, though a single glance, almost, would have revealed her had anything like a careful search of the flower beds close to the house been made, no one came near her hiding-place. Between her and the open garden was only a flimsy screen of rose bushes, but it proved enough.

She stayed there, scarcely daring to breathe, while the men searched the grounds and the beach. And she was still there, more than an hour later, when they returned, tired and discouraged, to report the failure of their search to Holmes, who was back in the room from which she had escaped.

"Fury!" cried Holmes. "She must be on the island! There's no way that she can have got away! Well, watch the boats! That will have to do for to-night. She can't get away without a boat—and they are all in the boat-house. If she wanders down to the other end, to the fort, we can catch her in the morning They won't believe any story she can tell them, if she should happen to get there. And I don't want to disturb them to-night—I'd rather wait until morning, when they will be over with the papers. I haven't any real right to hold them to-night, except the right of force."

Bessie thrilled at the information those few words gave her. She remembered now that there was a fort, manned by United States soldiers, on

Humber Island. It was one of the chain of forts
that guarded the approaches to Rock Haven. And
Bessie had an idea that she would be able to find
someone at the fort to believe her story, wild and
improbable as she knew it must sound. The great
problem now was to get out of the grounds unseen.

And that problem, of course, her cleverness in
hiding so close to the house had made much easier
to solve. No one would suspect now that she was
there; if she waited until the house was quiet, and
the men who were to watch the boats had gone
to their post, she should be able to steal out of the
garden and in the direction of the fort.

To be on the safe side, she waited nearly an hour
longer. Then, as quietly as she could, she began
her solitary walk. Fortune, and her own ability
to move quietly, favored her. In five minutes she
was out of the grounds, and in woods where,
though the walking was difficult, and she stumbled
more than once, she at least felt safe from the
danger of pursuit.

Soon the woods began to thin; then they grew

thicker again. But, after she had been walking, as she guessed, for more than an hour, it grew lighter and she saw ahead of her the outlines of dark buildings—Fort Humber, she was sure. And a minute later the sharp hail of a sentry halted her, and at the same time made her sure that she had not lost her way.

"Who goes there?" called the sentry.

"I've lost my way," said Bessie, trusting to her voice to make him understand that she was not to be driven away. "Is this the fort? I'd like to see some officer, if you please."

"Wait there! I'll pass the word," said the sentry.

And in a few minutes a young lieutenant came toward her.

"Bless my soul!" he said. "What are you doing here, young lady? Come with me—you can explain inside."

And, once inside the fort, the first person she saw was Charlie Jamieson!

CHAPTER XIV

"Bessie King!" he exclaimed amazed. "What on earth are you doing here? And where is Trenwith?"

"I don't know," said Bessie. She felt safe and for a moment she was on the verge of collapsing completely. But then she remembered that not her own fate alone, but that of the others whom she loved and who had been so good to her depended upon her. And, in a few quick words, she told the story of the accident to the *Columbia*, with the treachery of Billy Trenwith and the subsequent appearance of Holmes and his men.

"There you are, gentlemen!" said Jamieson, turning to the little group of men in uniform, who, tremendously interested, had listened intently to all that Bessie had said. "You laughed at me—

you insisted that the sort of thing I told you about wasn't possible—that it simply couldn't happen in this country, and in this time. What do you think now?"

"I guess it's one on us," said one of the officers, with a reluctant laugh. "But, really, Jamieson, you can't blame us much, can you? It's pretty incredible, even now."

"I'm bothered about Trenwith, though," said Charlie "Something has gone wrong."

"Miss Mercer is perfectly sure that he is in league with Mr. Holmes," said Bessie. "Do you think that's so, Mr. Jamieson?"

"I hope not," said Charlie, soberly. "I've found out one thing lately though, Bessie;—that when there is money involved, you can never tell what is going to happen."

"Did you know we were here—how did you find out?"

"No questions just now! It's time something was being done. Tell me, can you take me to this house, and show me how to get in?"

"Yes, I think I can find my way back through the woods."

"No need of that," said one of the officers. "There's a road that leads right to that place. What's Holmes doing there, anyhow? It isn't his place It belongs to some people who bought it a little while ago."

"Yes, a Mr. and Mrs. Richards," said Charlie. "But from what Bessie here says, he seems to be doing about as he likes with it. Well, I don't want to waste any more time. Do you suppose I can see Colonel Hart?"

"You can unless your eyesight is failing," said the Colonel, appearing in the doorway. He had heard the question, and came forward smiling, his hand outstretched. "How are you, Jamieson? What can I do for you?"

"A great deal, if you will, Colonel," said Charlie. "I'd like to speak to you privately for a minute, if I may—"

"Shabby business—that's what I call it," said one of the young officers. "He knows we're wild

to know what's going on, and there he goes off
with the old man to tell him about it where we
can't hear."

Then one of them happened to think that Bessie
might be in need of refreshment after her exciting experiences, and they waited on her as if she
had been a princess. By the time she had been
able to convince them that she wanted nothing
more, Jamieson and the Colonel returned.

"All right, my boy," the colonel was saying.
"I'll attend to it, and do as you wish. Maybe
it isn't strictly according to the regulations,
but I don't believe anyone will ever file charges
against me. Depend upon me. You're starting
now?"

"Yes," said Jamieson   "Come along, Bessie.
We're going back to the house "

"I'm ready," said Bessie, simply.

"You're not afraid?"

"Not as long as you're there. I don't believe
Mr Holmes can do anything while you're around."

"Well, I hope he can't, Bessie. But when they

had managed to get away as you did to-night, a whole lot of girls wouldn't be in a hurry to run into the same danger again "

"I wouldn't be very happy about getting away myself unless Zara escaped, too, Mr. Jamieson. And I'm afraid of Mr. Holmes—I don't know what he might do if he were angry enough. I wouldn't be sure that Dolly and Miss Eleanor were safe with him."

"Well, they are, Bessie. Of course, what I'm planning may go wrong, but I feel pretty confident that we are going to give Mr. Holmes the surprise of his life this night."

They walked on steadily through the darkness, the going of course being much easier than Bessie had found it in her flight, since she now had a good road under her feet instead of the stumpy wood path, full of twisted roots and unexpected bumps.

And at last a light showed through the trees to one side of the road, and Bessie stopped.

"That's the place, I'm pretty sure," she said.

"I can tell for certain if we turn in, but I'm sure I didn't pass another house."

So they went in, and a minute's examination enabled Bessie to recognize the grounds. She had had plenty of time to study them earlier in the night, when she had crouched behind the rose bushes, expecting to be discovered and dragged out every time one of the searchers passed near her.

"I wish I knew about Trenwith," said Charlie, anxiously. "That is one part of this night's work that puzzles me. I don't understand it at all, and it worries me."

"He went off with Mr. Holmes after we got inside the house," said Bessie. "But I didn't see him again after that. He wasn't with Mr. Holmes in the big hall again, after I had got away. I'm sure of that"

"What are you going to do now?" asked Bessie.

"I'm not certain I'd like very much to know where the other girls are. We ought to be all together."

"Perhaps I can find out," said Bessie. "You stay here, and I'll slip along toward the house. If Dolly's awake, I can find out where she is."

"All right. But if you see anyone else, or if anyone interferes with you, call me right away"

Bessie promised that she would, and then she slipped away, and a moment later found herself in front of the house.

"I'll try this side last," she said to herself. "I don't believe they'd put them in front—more likely they'd put them on the east side, because that only looks out over the garden, and there'd be less chance of their seeing anyone who was coming."

So, moving stealthily and as silently as a cat, she went around to that side of the house, and a moment later the strange, mournful call of a whip-poor-will sounded in the still night air. It was repeated two or three times, but there was no answer. Then Bessie changed her calling slightly.

At first she had imitated the bird perfectly. But this time there was a false note in the call—just the slightest degree off the true pitch of the bird's

6—C15

note. Most people would not have known the
difference, but to a trained ear that slight imper-
fection would be enough to reveal the fact that
it was a human throat that was responsible, and
not a bird's. And the trick served its turn, for
there was an instant answer. A window was
opened above Bessie, very gently, and she saw
Dolly's head peering down over the ivy that grew
up the wall

"Wait there!" she whispered   "Get dressed,
all three of you! Mr. Jamieson is here—not far
away. I'm going to tell him where you are."

She marked the location of the window care-
fully, and then, sure that she would remember it
when she returned, went back to Jamieson

"Did you locate them? Good work!" he said.
"All right. Go back now and tell them to make a
rope of their sheets—good and strong. I saw
where you were standing, and, if they lower that,
I don't think we will have any trouble getting up
to their window. I want to be inside that house—
and I don't want Holmes to know I'm there until

I'm ready " He chuckled "He thinks I'm back
in the city. I want him to have a real surprise
when he finally does see me "

Bessie slipped back then and told Dolly what
to do, and in a few minutes the rope of sheets came
down, rustling against the ivy. Bessie made the
signal she had agreed on with Jamieson at once—
a repetition of the bird's call, and he joined
her Then he picked her up and started her
climbing up the wall, with the aid of the rope and
the ivy.

For a girl as used to climbing trees as Bessie,
it was a task of no great difficulty, and in a minute she was safely inside the room, and had turned
to watch Jamieson following her. His greater
weight made his task more difficult, and twice those
above had all they could do to repress screams of
terror, for the ivy gave way, and he seemed certain
to fall.

But he was a trained athlete, and a skillful
climber as well, and, difficult as the ascent proved
to be for him, he managed it, and clambered over

the sill of the window and into the room, breathless, but smiling and triumphant.

"Oh, I'm so glad you're here, Charlie!" said Eleanor. "There is someone we can trust, after all, isn't there?"

"Oh, sure!" he said. "Don't you take on, Nell, and don't ask a lot of questions now. It'll be daylight pretty soon—and, believe me, when the light comes, there's going to be considerable excitement around these parts."

"But why did you bring Bessie back here? How did she find you?"

He raised his hand with a warning gesture, and smiled

"Remember, Nell, no questions!" he said "All we can do just now is to wait."

Wait they did—and in silence, save for an occasional whisper.

"That man Holmes has a woman guarding us," whispered Eleanor. "She is just outside the door in the hall—sleeping there. The idea is to keep us from leaving these rooms. Evidently they never thought of our going by the window. We did think of it, but we couldn't see any use in it, because we felt we wouldn't know where to go on this island, even if we got outside the grounds!"

"That's what he counted on, I guess," answered Charlie. "I'm glad you stayed. Cheer up, Nell! You're going to have a package of assorted surprises before you're very much older!"

To the five of them, practically imprisoned, it seemed as if daylight would never come. But at last a faint brightness showed through the window, and gradually the objects in the room became more distinct. And, with the coming of the light, there came also sounds of life in the house. The voices of men sounded from the garden, and Charlie smiled.

"They'll begin wondering about that rope and footprints under this window pretty soon," he said. "And I guess none of them will be exactly anxious to tell Holmes, either."

He was right, for in a few moments excited

voices echoed from below, and then there was an argument.

"Well, he's got to be told," said one man. "It's your job, Bill."

"Suppose you do it yourself."

Apparently, they finally agreed to go together. And five minutes later there was a commotion outside the door.

"Here's where I take cover!" whispered Charlie, with a grin And, just before the door was opened, and Holmes burst in, his face livid with anger, the lawyer hid himself behind a closet door.

Holmes started at the sight of the four girls standing there, fully dressed, his jaw dropping

"So you're all here?" he said, an expression of relief gradually succeeding his consternation. "Found you couldn't get away, eh, Bessie? Why didn't you come to the front door instead of climbing in that way? We'd have let you in all right." He laughed, harshly.

"Well, I've had about all the trouble you're going to give me," he said. "Silas Weeks will be here to take care of you pretty soon, my girl, and now that he's got you in the state where you belong, I guess you won't get away again very soon "

"What state do you think this island is in?" asked Charlie Jamieson, appearing suddenly from his hiding-place

Holmes staggered back For a moment he seemed speechless Then he found his tongue.

"What are you doing here? How did you get into my house?" he snarled. "I'll have you arrested as a burglar "

"Ah, no, you won't," said Charlie, pleasantly. "But I'm going to have you arrested—for kidnapping Answer my question—do you think this is in the state where the courts have put Bessie in charge of Silas Weeks?"

"Certainly it is," said Holmes, blustering

"You ought to keep up with the news better, Mr. Holmes The United States Government has bought this island for military purposes It's a Federal reservation now, and the writ of the state courts has no value whatever. Even the land this house stands on belongs to the government now— it was taken by condemnation proceedings.''

Eleanor gave a glad cry at the good news. At last she understood the trap into which Holmes had fallen.

''Look outside—look through the window!'' said Jamieson.

Holmes rushed to the window, and his teeth showed in a snarl at what he saw.

''You can't get away, you see,'' said Jamieson. ''There isn't any sentiment about those soldiers. They'd shoot you if you tried to run through them. I'd advise you to take things easily. There'll be a United States marshal to take you in charge pretty soon. He's on his way from Rock Haven now. He'll probably come on the same boat that brings Silas Weeks—and some other people you are not expecting.''

Holmes slumped into a chair. Defeat was written in his features. But he pulled himself together presently.

"You've got the upper hand right now," he said. "But what good does it do you? I'm the only one who knows the truth, and the reason for all this. They won't do anything to me—they can't prove any kidnapping charge. The boat was disabled—I entertained these girls over night when they were stranded here."

"We'll see about that," said Jamieson, quietly. "And I may know more than you think. I've been finding out a few things since the talk I had with Jake Hoover in Bay City yesterday. Did you know that he was arrested the day before yesterday at Plum Beach?"

Evidently Holmes had not known it. The news was a fresh shock to him. But he was determined not to admit defeat.

"Much good he'll do you!" he said. "He doesn't know anything—even if he thinks he does."

CHAPTER XV.

THE MYSTERY SOLVED

There was a knock at the door, and, in answer to Jamieson's call to come in, one of the young officers Bessie had seen at the fort entered. He smiled cheerfully at Bessie, saluted the other girls, and grinned at Jamieson.

"We've herded all the people we found around the place down in the boat-house," he said. "They were too scared to do anything. Is this your man Holmes?"

"You guessed right the very first time, Lieutenant," said Charlie. "Any sign of that boat from Rock Haven?"

"She's just coming in," said the officer. "She ought to land her passengers at the pier in about ten minutes."

"Then it's time to go down to meet her," said Charlie. "Come on, girls, and you too, Holmes

You'll be needed down there. And I guess you'll
find it worth your while to come, too ''

Holmes, protesting, had no alternative, and in
sullen silence he was one of the little group that
now made its way toward the pier. She was
just being tied up as they arrived, and Silas
Weeks, his face full of malign triumph at the
sight of Bessie and Zara, was the first to step
ashore.

"Got yer, have I?" he said. He turned to a
lanky, angular man who was at his side. "There
y'are, constable," he said. "There's yer parties
—them two girls there! Arrest them, will yer?"

"Not here, I won't," said the constable. "You
didn't tell me it was to come off here. This is
government land—I ain't got no authority here."

"You keep your mouth shut and your eyes and
ears open, Weeks," said Jamieson, before the
angry old farmer could say anything. Then he
stepped forward to greet a man and woman who
had followed Weeks down the gangplank.

"I'm glad you're here, Mrs. Richards, and you

too, Mr. Richards," he said. "I'm going to be able to keep my promise."

Holmes was staring at Mrs Richards and her husband in astonishment

"You here, Elizabeth?" he exclaimed "And Henry, too? I didn't know you were coming!"

"We decided to come quite unexpectedly, Morton," said the lady, quietly She was a woman of perhaps forty-two or three, tall and distinguished in her appearance. But, like her husband, her face showed traces of privations and hardship.

Behind them came a stiff, soldierly looking man, in a blue suit, and him Jamieson greeted with a smile and handshake.

"There's your man, marshal," he said, pointing to Holmes. "I guess he won't make any resistance."

And, while Mr. and Mrs. Richards stared in astonishment, and Weeks turned purple, the marshal laid his hand on the merchant's shoulder, and put him under arrest. Holmes was trapped at last.

"What does this mean?" Mrs Richards asked, indignantly. "What are you doing to my brother, Mr. Jamieson?"

"That's quite a long story, Mrs Richards," he answered, easily. "And, strange as it may seem, I'll have to answer it by asking you and your husband some questions that may seem very personal But I've made good with you so far, and I can assure you that you will have no cause to regret answering me."

Mrs. Richards bowed.

"In the first place, you and your husband have been away from this part of the country for quite a long time, haven't you?"

"Yes For a number of years "

"And you have not always been as well off, financially, as you are now?"

"That is quite true My husband, shortly after our marriage, failed in business, owing—owing to conditions he couldn't control "

"Isn't it true, Mrs. Richards, that those conditions were the result of his marriage to you?

Didn't your father, a very rich man, resent your marriage so deeply that he tried to ruin your husband in order to force you to leave him?''

There were tears in the woman's eyes as she nodded her head in answer.

''Thank you. I know this is very painful—but I must really do all this. You refused to leave your husband, however, and when he decided to go to Alaska, you went with him?

''And there he made a lucky strike, some four or five years ago, that made him far richer than he had ever dreamed of becoming?''

''That is quite true.''

''But, although you were rich, you did not come home? You spent a good deal of time in the Far North, and when you went out for a rest, you came no further east than Seattle or San Francisco?''

''There was no reason for us to come here. All our friends had turned against us in our misfortunes, and our only child was dead. So it was only a few months ago that we came home.''

''That is very tragic   Thank you, Mrs. Richards. One moment—I have another question to ask "

He stepped toward the gangplank.

"I will be back in a moment," he said

He went on board the boat, and while all those on the dock, puzzled and mystified by his questions, waited, he disappeared. When he returned he was not alone A woman was with him, and, at the sight of her Bessie gave a cry of astonishment

"Now, Mrs Richards," said Charlie. "Have you ever seen this woman before?"

"I think I have," she said, in a strange, puzzled tone "But—she has changed so—"

"Her name is Mrs. Hoover, Mrs Richards. Does that help you to remember?"

"Oh!" Mrs Richards sobbed and burst into tears "Mrs. Hoover!" she said, brokenly. "To think that I could forget you! Tell me—"

"One moment," said Charlie, interrupting His own voice was not very steady, and Eleanor, a look of dawning understanding in her eyes, was staring at him, greatly moved   "It was with Mrs. Hoover that you left your child when you went west under an assumed name, was it not? It was she who told you that she had died?"

"Oh, I lied to you—I lied to you!" wailed Maw Hoover, breaking down suddenly, and throwing herself at the feet of Mrs Richards. "She wasn't dead   It was that wicked Mr. Holmes and Farmer Weeks who made me say she was."

"What?" thundered Richards. "She isn't dead? Where is she?"

"Bessie!" said Charlie, calling to her sharply. "Here is your daughter, Mrs. Richards, and a daughter to be proud of!"

And the next moment Bessie, Bessie King, the waif no longer, but Bessie Richards, was in her mother's arms!

"So Mr. Holmes was Bessie's uncle!" said Eleanor, amazed. "But why did he act so?"

"I can explain that," said Charlie, sternly. "It was he who set his father so strongly against his sister's marriage to Mr. Richards. He expected

that he would inherit, as a result, her share of his
father's estate, as well as his own But his plans
miscarried. Mrs Richards and her husband had
disappeared before her father's death, and, when
he softened and was inclined to relent, he could
not find them But he knew they had a daughter,
and he left to her his daughter's share of his fortune—over a million dollars. There was no trace
of the child, however, and so there was a provision
in the will that if she did not come forward to claim
the money on her eighteenth birthday it should go
to her uncle—to Holmes.''

"I always said it was money that was making
him act that way!" cried Dolly Ransom.

"Yes," said Jamieson. "He had squandered
much of his own money—he wanted to make sure
of getting Bessie's fortune for himself. So when
he learned through Silas Weeks where the child
was, he paid Mrs. Hoover to tell her parents she
was dead, and then, after she had run away, he
and Weeks did all they could to get her back to a
place where there was no chance of anyone find-

ing out who she was   They nearly succeeded—
but I have been able to block their plans   And
one reason is that they were greedy and they
couldn't let Zara Slavin and her father alone.
He is a great inventor and they profited by his
ignorance of American customs.''

''I only found out her name last night,''
said Eleanor   ''I wondered if he could be the
Slavin who invented the new wireless telephone—''

''They got him into jail on a trumped-up
charge,'' said Charlie   ''And then they tried to
keep Zara away from people who might learn the
truth from her, and offer to supply the money he
needed.   In a little while they would have robbed
him of all the profits of his invention ''

''I'll finance it myself,'' said Richards, ''and he
can keep all of the profit.''

Bessie's father and mother were far too glad
to get her back to want to punish Ma Hoover,
who was sincerely repentant.   They could hardly
find words enough to thank Eleanor and Dolly for

their friendship, and to Charlie Jamieson their gratitude was unbounded.

But suddenly, even while the talk was at its height, there was a diversion. Billy Trenwith, his clothes torn, his hands chafed and bleeding, appeared on the dock.

"Good Heavens, Billy, I'd forgotten all about you!" said Charlie. "Where have you been?"

"How can you speak to him as a friend after the way he betrayed us?" asked Eleanor, indignantly, and Billy winced. But Charlie laughed happily.

"He didn't betray you," said he. "I cooked up this whole thing, just to catch Holmes red-handed, and he walked right into the trap. I told Billy not to tell you, because I wanted you to act so that Holmes wouldn't know it was a trick"

"He didn't trust me, though," said Billy, ruefully. "As soon as he had the girls, he tied me up and chucked me into his cellar so that I couldn't change my mind, he said. That's why I didn't meet you at the fort."

Eleanor, shamefaced and miserable, looked at

him. Then, with tears in her eyes, she held out her hand to him.

"Can you ever forgive me?" she asked.

"You bet I can!" he shouted. "Why, you were meant to think just what you did! There's nothing to forgive!"

"I ought to have known you couldn't do a mean, treacherous thing," she said.

"All's well that ends well," said Charlie, gaily. "Now as to your brother, Mrs. Richards? I don't suppose you want him arrested?"

"No—oh, no!" said she, looking at Holmes contemptuously.

"Then, if you'll withdraw the charge of kidnapping, Eleanor, he can go."

And the next moment Holmes, free but disgraced, slunk away, and out of the lives of those he had so cruelly wronged.

*   *   *   *   *

Sunset of that day found them all back at Plum Beach, where the Camp Fire Girls, who had been almost frantic at their long absence, greeted them with delight. The story of Bessie's restoration to her parents, and of the good fortune that was soon to be Zara's, seemed to delight the other girls as much as if they themselves were the lucky ones, and Gladys Cooper, completely restored to health, was the first to kiss Bessie and wish her joy.

And after dinner Eleanor, blushing, rose to make a little speech.

"You know, girls," she said, "Margery Burton is to be a Torch-Bearer as soon as we get back to the city. And you are going to need a new Guardian soon She will be chosen—and she will make a better one than I have been, I think "

There was a chorus of astonished cries

"But why are you going to stop being Guardian, Miss Eleanor?" asked Margery.

" Because—because— "

"I'll tell you why," said Billy Trenwith, leaping up and standing beside her. "It's because she's going to be married to me!"

There was a moment of astonished silence.

And then, from every girl there burst out, without signal, the words of the Camp Fire song:

"Wo-he-lo —wo-he-lo —wo he-lo —Wo-he-lo for Love!"

www.ingramcontent.com/pod-product-compliance
Lightning Source LLC
Chambersburg PA
CBHW020800250626
47155CB00003B/1161